D1431095

THE BLONDE WORE BLACK

When two slugs put paid to him out on Indian Point, Poetry Brookman had eight thousand reasons to worry, and having a dumb name wasn't one of them. Turns out he owned bookie Jake the Take Martello in a big way. Naturally, Jake wanted both his dough and some answers: enter Private Detective Mark Preston to sniff around the losers and bruisers.

Preston runs into some oddballs: arts promoter Hugo Somerset, and his lithe protégé Flower; there's chisel-chinned Clyde Hamilton, clean-cut hoodlum; two-bit thug Legs McCann, looking for the exit sign; and beatific Eve Prince, on the wrong end of a blackmail sting after a piano recital hits the wrong note. Preston would like to know her a little better. . .

The stakes are high, the double-cross lurks and every bullet has a name on it—but Mark Preston isn't one to walk away from trouble.

THE BLONDE WORE BLACK

Peter Chambers

·BLACK·
DAGGER
CRIME·

First Published 1968
by
Robert Hale Ltd

This edition 1999 by Chivers Press
published by arrangement with
the author

ISBN 0 7540 8539 2

British Library Cataloguing in Publication Data available

Printed and bound in Great Britain by
Redwood Books, Trowbridge, Wiltshire

CHAPTER ONE

I never heard of Poetry Brookman till the day they found him smashed up on the rocks below Indian Point. Even then he didn't rate too much space, just one half column on the front page of the Bugle. It's tricky up there on the point, and we get an average of two or three people every year winding up at the bottom. Some are plain suicides, some plain unlucky, caught in the sudden alarming gusts of wind which are a peculiarity of the place.

So I wasn't too interested in Brookman, despite the fancy name. After noting that he was thirty-one years old, and a poet—that was a twist—I got down to the serious reading. I was half way through a biased report on the game the Buffaloes played the preceding evening when Florence Digby came in. Shuffling feverishly at the papers, I tried to get the financial section to the top before she reached the desk.

Her frosty and knowing smile told me I was wasting my time.

"There is a client here, if you're not too busy Mr. Preston."

"What kind of client?"

La Digby always seems to be on the winning team in this private war we have. An employer ought to get more respect.

"His name is Clyde F. Hamilton. A business counsellor," she added portentously.

Anybody listening was permitted to assume that a business counsellor was a person of position, and entitled to some respect. He was not under any circumstances to be bracketed with persons of low repute and intellect, particularly people like private investigators.

"Usher the gentleman in," I said loftily.

She went and held open the door.

"Will you come in, Mr. Hamilton?"

He came in young and confident, treating Florence to a half-bow as he passed. She swept out feeling like a queen. I took a look at my visitor. He was in his middle twenties, and everything about him, from the handsome close-cropped head to the hand-made tooled leather shoes shouted Ivy League.

"How are you Mr. Preston?"

We shook hands and he lowered himself into a chair with the grace of a trained athlete.

"Football?" I queried.

He laughed, and it was a pleasant sight.

"Not any more. I played a lot in my college days, but I just missed out on All-American. After that I let it drop. Nowadays it's just a little track work and a spell in the gym now and then."

"So it isn't any use my offering you a cigaret," I said.

I stuck an Old Favorite in my face and had another look at him through the flame of the lighter. There was something about the open clean cut face that I didn't care for, but I was probably just being unreasonable. Or plain jealous.

"I have a feeling you're not a Monkton man," I told him. "Not that I know everybody in town."

"No, you're absolutely right. I'm from all over. My business takes me over half the country. Right now I'm having a short spell in your city. Liking it, too. There's some fine swimming."

6

Instinctively I glanced out of the window towards the sparkling blue of the Pacific.

"Yeah," I admitted regretfully. "Trouble is, it tends to make it all the more difficult to stick to work, when other people are splashing around out there."

Which led us nicely, I hoped, away from the pleasantries and into the hard facts of whatever was troubling Clyde F. Hamilton.

"Perhaps I should tell you why I'm here," he began. "The fact is, I'm little more than a messenger. A client of mine would like you to call and see him."

"O.K. What about?"

He made deprecatory faces.

"I'm afraid that's something he would have to discuss with you direct."

"Fair enough. What's his name?"

I had a pencil over a nice clean sheet of paper. People prefer it when you take notes. It looks more professional.

"Mr. J. J. Martello," he said carefully.

I put the pencil down incredulously.

"Jake the Take Martello?" I asked.

He frowned, and suddenly his lips were much thinner.

"Mr. Martello's given name is Jacob. I don't much care for gutter nicknames, nor for people who use them."

Jake Martello was one of the biggest bookmakers in town. A one-time barber, who made book on the side, he had grown steadily bigger for twenty years, and the lather brush was a long way behind him now. And now I realized what it was about Hamilton. The old-style mobster with the blue shave and the fedora hat was a figure in a history book. The big organization men now hired young college guys like Hamilton, people with appearance and background, people who could mix in

7

any circles. But they don't impress me. You can give a rat a shave and a three hundred dollar suit, and to me he still stinks of the sewers. I was all through smiling at Mr. Hamilton.

"Nobody's interested in what you care about," I assured him. "You said you were a messenger boy. Well, get it said and get out."

His smile was even thinner and there was death in his eyes.

"I must be sure to remember that, Mr. Preston. And I've told you why I came. Mr. Martello wants you to see him."

"Can't he pay his telephone bill?" I demanded.

He stood up.

"It would take a better man than you to make me lose my temper," he assured me. "As for telephones, they are not suitable for delicate business matters. When will you call on Mr. Martello?"

I yawned, and looked at my watch.

"Where will he be around noon?"

"He is normally at a place called the Oyster's Cloister at noon. Mr. Martello usually takes coffee and brandy at that hour."

"I'll get down there if I can."

He nodded coldly and went out. Before I'd picked up the newspaper, Florence Digby was back.

"What did you say to Mr. Hamilton," she queried indignantly. "He didn't even say good morning."

"You ought not to judge by appearances, Miss Digby. Your nice young man is a thug. A well-dressed, well-spoken thug, but a thug just the same."

She sniffed in evident disbelief, and went away. I was intrigued to know what Jake Martello wanted with me. He could hire a small army if he wanted, and I didn't see what I could do that they couldn't. There was just one

8

comfort. It had to be something legal. Jake would never look at an outsider for the other kind of work.

I parked half a block away from the Oyster's Cloister and walked the rest. The place is run by a friend of mine, Reuben Krantz, and I hadn't given him a play in months. The Cloister has a jealous reputation for its fine cuisine, and people said the chef, Armand, was the highest paid chef in the city, if not along the entire coast. In the ordinary way, the eating prices are out of my bracket, but there's a pleasant bar attached. It's one of those spots where you can imagine you're wealthy for the price of a scotch and soda, watching other people diving into the twelve fifty filet mignon. It is one of those little peculiarities of life that Krantz personally is unable to join in on the eating spree. He has this stomach condition that normally restricts him to simple plain foods. One of his excesses is a special brew of pigs knuckles, and this is where he and Armand differ. The chef maintains he is not employed to boil up swill, and simply will not deliver knuckles, special recipe or no. So if you happen to be passing the Oyster's Cloister one evening around nine thirty, you may be in time to see a steaming dish being carried over from the delicatessen across the street.

The doorman is a big husky named Biff, and his leathery face split open when he saw me.

"Well well Mr. Preston. I thought maybe you left town."

"Hi, Biff. Boss around?"

"In the office." He patted at his stomach. "It's not one of those good days."

"Thanks for the tip."

I went through the glass doors and peeked in the bar. There were four or five people in there, none familiar. Then I tapped on the door marked "Manager".

"Come in."

9

Krantz was seated behind his green leather-topped desk. Beside the wall was a table with a crystal water jug, and enough pills and powders in heaped boxes to stock a small druggists.

"Don't tell me, don't tell me—I have the name on the tip of my tongue," he greeted.

"Hallo Ben. I've been busy lately, thought it was time I looked in."

"It is, it is," he confirmed. "How're things?"

We chatted away about this and that for a few minutes. Then he suddenly clutched at his stomach and an expression of resigned agony came over his face.

"No improvement huh?" I asked.

He shook his head and waited till the spasm passed.

"I tell you, there's an overnight fortune for the guy who really finds out how to deal with these things."

"I imagine. I was talking to a guy a month or two back who did something with seaweed."

His eyes brightened.

"Seaweed huh? You remember the details?"

"No," I confessed. "But next time I see him I'll get him to tell me what it's all about."

He nodded eagerly.

"Fine. Make it soon huh? You want to call him from here?"

He began pushing a telephone forward.

"No thanks," I hedged, "I don't even know his number. But I'll get on it. By the way, I hear Jake Martello gets in here some mornings."

The brightness went from his eyes at the mention of the name, and the normal obscure look took its place.

"Sometimes. What about it?"

"Nothing. Just want to have a talk with him, that's all."

Now the whole face was suspicious.

"Talk? Not trouble talk? The Cloister ain't built for it."

"You know I wouldn't do anything like that here."

He wanted to say something but natural caution caused him to hesitate.

"Look Preston, Jake can be bad company if he don't get along with people. I'm running low on friends as it is."

And even in saying that much, Krantz was coming further out of his shell for me than most people would see him do in a lifetime. And he'd done it for me before.*

I grinned and shook my head.

"Thanks Ben, but this is just routine. Anyway, nice to see you."

We shook hands, and he reminded me of my promise to get him the seaweed prescription. Then I left him brooding over which pill to try today, and went out to the bar.

The early drinkers looked at me incuriously, in that casual impersonal way peculiar to early morning bar-flies. I walked through and looked into the restaurant. Only two tables were in use that early, and at one of them a young fellow was talking earnestly to a woman ten years older. The table in the far corner was the one for me. Martello sat with his back to the wall. Next to him was another man his own age, a stranger. The third man was my earlier visitor, Hamilton. Opening the door, I trod the deep carpeted steps down inside. The head waiter swept up, smile becoming a little fixed when he saw who it was.

"Hallo Ernie. I don't need a table thanks. I'll join Mr. Martello."

He nodded and escorted me across the small dance floor. Martello saw me coming and waved. When I reached him

* *Nobody Lives Forever.*

the other man looked at me with interest. Hamilton just looked.

"Hi ya Preston. Long time no see."

Martello held out a soft pudgy hand sparkling with diamonds. I held it briefly.

"Hallo Jake. You wanted to see me."

"Sure, sure, they's plenty time. Why doncha siddown. Take a cuppa coffee maybe, little brandy?"

"I'll take the brandy, leave the coffee."

He sighed.

"So many people just don't know what's good. Coffee is good, brandy is good, fine. But together, man that's an experience."

To show he was a man who believed in his own theories, he tipped most of his brandy into the half empty coffee cup and gulped at the mixture. When he put down the cup his face was wreathed in smiles.

"That's a real breakfast," he beamed. "Oh say, I nearly forgot. This here's my brother Charl.. He's down from Frisco. You know Clyde." The brother nodded, Hamilton stared at the table, Charlie was not unlike Jake, fifty-ish black curly hair going thin on top, heavy jowled face that needed two shaves a day and got them. I'd never heard of any brother before, it might be worth having him looked up. His voice had the same nasal twang to it.

"We don't say Frisco, Mr. Preston, We say San Francisco. Only outsiders like Jake here say Frisco."

"I'll remember."

Jake chuckled.

"Always he tells me about it, always I forget. Some brandy for my guest here, the best in the house."

A waiter had materialized behind me and Jake waved him on his way. I noticed Hamilton was only drinking coffee.

"You on vacation, Mr. Martello?"

I knew Jake wouldn't talk until the waiter had carried out his mission, and I had to say something. Charlie nodded slowly.

"Kind of. Little family business, I like to keep in touch."

"That's the trouble with the world today," sighed Jake. "People don't have proper respect for the family no more. All these terrible things going on, they wouldn't happen if people paid attention to their families."

All I knew about Jake's family was that he had an uncle shot down in a bank stick-up back in the thirties. But this was not the occasion for little reminiscences of the kind.

"Guess that's true," I muttered.

My drink came then and I sipped at it.

"Luck," I said to Jake.

"Bottoms up," he counselled. "Now then, there's a little thing I'd like you to be looking at, Preston."

"What kind of thing?"

"There was a guy bumped off last night, or maybe early this morning. Name of Poetry Brookman, if you can believe it."

"Bumped off?" I queried. "It said in the paper he fell off Indian Point, or else he jumped."

"You musta caught an early edition," Jake told me. "Fact is the guy's head was all stoved in by them rocks. It wasn't till the doc got a good look at him they found there was two slugs in his head. The back of his head."

"All right, somebody knocked him off. What about it?"

Jake leaned forward, his voice little more than a whisper.

"This about it. This Brookman was in to me for nearly eight grand. Today is payday. Only Jake don't get no payday. And I don't like that."

Now it was clearer. In the bookie business you don't

get to be a big name like Martello by having people go around welshing on you. Not even corpses.

"You got the message now?" he asked.

"Sure. You want me to dig around, find out who took care of him."

"Right."

"I hear tell we have a police force in town. You don't suppose they might do just as well without me?"

"Maybe. But to them this is just another number. In this fine city last year we had one hundred and sixty seven killings. That's better'n three a week. What chance has Homicide got with that little squad of theirs? The odds are way out."

"They have a good record," I pointed out.

"By comparison with other cities, sure. But they still come up with less than forty per cent answers. Those kinda odds are no use to me with this Brookman thing. You can hire all the help you need, spend whatever you want. Spread around plenty of the sugar. That's the kind of thing brings up answers. The cops can't do that."

"I can't guarantee results," I reminded.

"I know that. But I know you'll sure as hell try. And that's all I'm asking. Is it a deal?"

I took another sip at the brandy. The golden glow of the first was just beginning to spread through my body.

"You say spend money. With a thing like this I might even spend the eight grand."

He made a face of disgust.

"Eight grand. I'd spend that on a good dinner if I wanted. Spend it, spend eighty if you need. I want answers."

It wasn't a question of money. It was a matter of professional standing. Somebody had cost Jake the Take Martello money, and somebody had to be told what a bad idea that was.

"And suppose I get lucky?" I questioned. "What happens then?"

He flapped a hand and the sun struck colored sparks from the bedecked fingers.

"Maybe nothing. If it was personal, like you know his wife maybe, or some guy fighting over a broad, well that's O.K. I don't want to interfere with personal people. These things happen."

"And if it wasn't like that?"

His eyes became heavy and the voice was flat.

"If it was other people, then they have to be told about the eight g's. Some mob guys or like that, they'll have to be told. They'd pay most likely. No, I'm not really worried about personal people or hard guys. What I want to know is, where's the dough? If this Brookman had it ready, it just could be somebody figured to take it away from him. That's the guy I want, the one who stole my money."

"He may not have known it was yours."

"Maybe. It don't make no difference. I want it back."

Hamilton spoke for the first time.

"I get the feeling Mr. Preston doesn't have the stomach for this type of operation."

"You step out back a moment and we'll talk some more," I replied nastily.

Martello chuckled briefly, his brother merely watched.

"Boys, boys," sighed Jake. "Anybody'd think you fellers couldn't get along."

"You better tell the pretty boy not to needle me, or I'll spread him over some alley," I warned.

Jake patted Hamilton on the arm as he was about to speak.

"Calm down. Clyde here is new in town. He don't

know about you, Preston." Turning to Hamilton he said, "Preston's O.K. He does what he does and he keeps his mouth shut."

"Whatever you say, Mr. Martello."

Each word was forced unwillingly through the handsome mouth.

"That is absolutely right. Whatever I say. Well Preston, what's it gonna be?"

I was thinking about it.

"If I turn up this killer, how do I know you won't knock him off?"

"Because I tell you so. Me personal, Jake Martello. And I guess my word's been good enough around this village for twenty years or more." That was true. Jake was as good as his word, whether for good or bad.

"Mind you," he qualified, "I ain't saying the guy wouldn't get pushed around some. People has to be taught manners when they mess in my business."

"No objections," I replied. "I don't like guys who shoot from behind anyway."

"Then it's a deal?" he beamed.

"I don't give guarantees," I repeated. "Let me try it for two days. If it comes up empty, I'll ask you whether you want to spend more money."

Jake turned to his brother.

"Ya see? Like I told you, this guy is on the level. You'll need some dough. Here."

He pulled a wadded roll of bills from his pocket.

"There's a grand, just to get you started. You need more, holler."

I got up, stuffing the roll in my pocket.

"After nine any evening at Rose's?"

He looked at my face to be certain I wasn't pulling his leg. Jake's admiration for Rose Suffolk was a byword in Monkton.

"Yeah, I get around there most nights," he nodded. "I'll be in touch."

The Martello brothers nodded. Hamilton studied the ceiling.

CHAPTER TWO

The oldest newspaper in town is the Monkton City Globe, and I went around to the office for a word with Shad Steiner. He was surrounded by the usual heaps of paper, and busy bawling somebody out over the telephone when I walked in.

"No," he was shouting, "There's no hurry, no hurry at all. We only print this magazine twice a year. You have thirty minutes to get that story in front of me."

The phone went down with a bang.

"Reporters," he scorned. "They call them reporters. I'd like to have seen a few of those bums covering the old 12th Ward thirty years ago. They'd have died of fright. What can I do for you, Preston? And why should I?"

"Now Shad, just calm down. It isn't my fault you have a bum staff."

He quivered with wrath.

"Bum staff? Who says I got a bum staff? Let me tell you, no newspaper in this town can match the Globe in any contest. And that includes staff. Anyway, what would a bar-haunting peeper know about real work, like running a newspaper?"

"I thought you said——"

"Never mind what I said. I don't have time to sit around flapping the breeze with you all day. State your business."

At least I needn't enquire after his health. When Steiner

barks and snaps that way, it means he is one hundred per cent fit.

"I noticed a few lines about the guy who fell off Indian Point today. Anything there for me?"

He squinted suspiciously over the top of his spectacles.

"You know something," he accused.

"No, I just don't happen to be working, and I wondered——"

"Don't lie to me. People have been trying for forty years and I always know. You got anything I can print?"

"No. But if I find out anything, I'll see you get it."

"H'm."

Diving into one of the heaps around him he fished out a sheet of paper.

"You might as well see this. Be on the street in two hours anyway."

It was a two column story now, with one-inch headlines. It confirmed what Martello had told me. What had seemed at first like natural causes turned out to be murder. Brookman lived alone at 824 Monteray Building and his occupation was poet. None had seen him later than eight o'clock the previous evening when he left the house of his friend, Hugo Somerset. Somerset was stated to be an entrepreneur, whatever that might be. He'd had a few friends in for drinks, one of them was Brookman. No, he didn't remember him leaving, nor whether anyone accompanied him. It sounded like that kind of party. There was a photograph, and obvious publicity handout, of a girl called Shiralee O'Connor, dancer. She'd been at the party too, presumably with more clothes on than the photograph indicated. In fairness to Somerset, if I had been present, I doubted whether I'd have known what time Brookman left either.

"Wow," I muttered.

Steiner chuckled.

"You should see some of the others her agent sent in. Sometimes I regret I'm such an old man."

"We'd soon see how old you are if she walked in here in this rig," I told him. "Who's working on this?"

"Randall, so far. They tell me Rourke is off with a head cold."

I didn't know whether that was good news or bad. Neither of them was much improvement on the other, from my point of view.

"You got anything you didn't print?" I demanded.

"The Globe prints all the facts," recited Steiner monotonously. "Our readers are entitled to know everything that happens."

"Don't stall me, Shad."

He whipped off the spectacles and tapped on the desk with them.

"The girl they call a dancer," he rapped. "She only dances the private circuit."

"Good. Anything else?"

"Got a list of the other people at the party. Here."

Another shuffle with the paper and he handed over a list of names. I didn't recognize any.

"Queer bunch," he submitted. "They're all poets, ballet dancers, composers nobody ever heard of. Fringe characters. I'll bet there isn't one with his rent paid up. Except this Somerset, of course. He seems to have plenty."

I made a note of Somerset's address. He'd need plenty to go with a neighborhood like that.

"I'm obliged to you Mr. Steiner. What was the name of this newspaper again? Maybe I'll buy one some day."

"We don't need it. Don't forget, if you come up with anything, it's mine."

"I'll remember."

Stuffing the names in my pocket, I went back out into

the street. It was almost one o'clock and my stomach was muttering something about food. I knew a place where I could grab a sandwich and maybe spend some of Martello's talk money at the same time.

I went to the Dutchman's, a place off Conquest Street where a man can get a schooner of beer and something to eat. You can also get more free advice in the Dutchman's than any other place I know. It is a hang-out for the horse players, that trusting band of citizens who are going to get rich tomorrow. And I'm not speaking about people who take an occasional interest in the ponies. These are the real players, the ones who eat sleep and talk nothing but nags, nags, nags. They know what's running in every race at every track, every day. They have all the inside stories, all the stable gossip, the conditions of every blade of grass at the track. The only thing they lack is the plain horse sense to notice that they're on the losing end ninety per cent of the time. They don't get rich, just old. They are one class of citizen who are always in need of money, either to pay out on losses already achieved, or to put down on the next race.

The guy I was looking for is one of these. Everybody calls him Charlie Surprise, although his real name is Suprosetti, or thereabouts. All I know for sure is that nobody could ever pronounce it, so he got stuck with Surprise.

As I walked in the door a thin unhappy looking man saw me at once, and sidled up.

"Hi, Mr. Preston."

"Hi, Mournful," I replied. "Say have you seen——"

"Listen, I know why you're here," he dropped his voice a whole octave, and I had to shove my ear almost against his mouth to get the rest. "I know Mr. Preston, and you are absolutely right."

"I am?"

'Sure. It's a boatrace. You don't imagine Wheeler wasted all that time running this nag in sticks tournaments? Of course you don't. And you're absolutely right. The whole thing is a boatrace. Hey, Mr. Preston, how's about putting on five for old Mournful? I mean lookit, did I ever steer you wrong?"

"Well, I guess not——" I began.

"Sure, I didn't. And would I start now for a lousy five bucks? Naturally not. Well, whaddya say?"

"What time is the race Mournful?"

His face dropped and all interest left his voice.

"You're putting me on. You don't even know what I'm talking about."

"Right," I confirmed. "Still, if five is going to save your life, here."

I stuffed a note in his hand, and he shook his head in disbelief.

"Such things don't happen. What do I have to do?"

"Nothing. It's my birthday. Just tell me where Charlie is and then go make a fortune."

He looked over my shoulder and the distant echo of a smile flitted across his face. With Mournful Harris, that is the equivalent of a great belly laugh from anyone else.

"Sure. He's right behind you."

I turned, and there he was coming through the door.

"Hey, Charlie."

He blinked nervously, and turned reluctantly towards the greeting. Your horseplayer is always expecting to hear from people he owes money.

"Oh it's you Mr. Preston. Listen, I'm pretty busy——"

"Let's go over and sit a while. You want a beer?"

I carried two schooners over to an empty corner. Charlie stood shuffling his pointed feet. I was glad of the poor light in the bar. In full daylight, Charlie can be very painful on the eyes. He was wearing a rainbow shirt with a screaming mauve collar, mustard colored pants and yellow shoes with a green stripe around the sides.

"Looking at you."

He dipped his sharp face into the foam and came up with bubbles all over his nose. Then he sat down abruptly.

"What's it all about, Mr. Preston?"

"It's about some folding money," I told him. "Just help me if you can, and you get some."

"Suddenly, I like the conversation."

He cheered up noticeably, and finally I had his attention.

"You ever hear of a guy named Brookman, Poetry Brookman?"

He rubbed anxiously at his nose.

"Brookman, Brookman."

"Had an address at the Monteray Building."

He shook his head.

"You're kidding about this Poetry tag, huh?"

"No. He was quite a horseplayer. Thought you were supposed to know all those guys."

Now I'd hurt his feelings.

"Sure I know 'em. I know everybody. And how do you mean, was? This Brookman ain't around any more?"

"He fell off Indian Point last night."

"Oh. That's too bad. Hey, wait a minute, would this be a skinny guy, kind of pale faced, looks like he oughta eat more?"

I'd never seen Brookman, and I wondered whether Charlie was dreaming up what he would normally expect anyone with a name like Poetry to look like.

"Could be. What about him?"

"There's been a guy around for a couple months looks like that. He's from outa town, and nobody knows him. But a player all right."

23

"What kind of age man would he be?"

"Who knows from birthdays?" he shrugged. "He wasn't no kid, but then again he wasn't nobody's grand-father."

Brookman had been thirty-one. At least Charlie's broad classification didn't exclude him.

"Tell me about him."

"Nothing to tell. He didn't talk to nobody, never made no trouble. A real student, though. I can tell."

It didn't sound as though Charlie was going to be much help.

"And you never saw anybody with him?" I pressed.

"No. At least, wait. Just hold on a little minute."

He screwed up his face in awful concentration.

"There was just the one time. It was, oh, weeks ago. I remember it struck me funny at the time. You know how it is, you keep seeing a guy around, all on his own lonesome. He never makes any contacts, never even passes the time of day. You get to thinking maybe he never does talk to anybody. A real loner. Then one day you see him with somebody. It's a surprise, you know what I mean?"

"I know what you mean. About this somebody, you have some idea who it was?"

"Oh sure. That's what struck me so funny, you know?"

Very patiently, I said.

"No Charlie, I don't know. Not yet. But if you'd like to come out with a name, then maybe we could all be surprised."

"Eh, oh sure. It was McCann."

He lowered his voice at the mention of the name, and I didn't blame him for that. Legs McCann was a man who didn't care for people shouting his name around.

"O.K. so I'm surprised," I conceded. "Where did you see them, what were they doing?"

"It was over at Palmtrees one day. They was just standing there, talking. Wasn't no more to it than that."

It could be enough, I reflected. The mere fact that Brookman might have known McCann was something worth a look. I put two fives on the table and skinny fingers scooped them up and pushed them out of sight.

"What does McCann do these days? I don't seem to be hearing too much about him lately."

Charlie's expression became wary.

"Lookit Mr. Preston, you know I like to help you if I can, and I can do with the bread. But I don't wanta have nothing to do with guys like that. I mean just to mention his name gives me the hives."

"Come on Charlie, I won't tell him."

He darted quick nervous glances all around the bar, then repeated the performance.

"I hear he's shacked up with some dame."

"That maybe, but they have to have groceries," I pointed out. "What else is he doing?"

"That's just it. Far as I know, the answer is nothing. It's like he retired or something."

"You wouldn't know who the woman is, or where they're staying?"

"Come on Mr. Preston, this ain't Information Please."

I put down another five and watched it disappear in the same direction as the others.

"Try to win a few huh, Charlie?"

I went out before he had a chance to explain at length just how he proposed to do that.

CHAPTER THREE

I went across town to the Monteray Building and headed for the manager's office. What I wanted was to get into the late Mr. Brookman's apartment and see what I could find. What the manager wanted was a reason for letting me in. I waved my license under his nose importantly.

"Looking for a guy who jumped his bond in Sacramento a year ago. He cost his company twenty thousand dollars, and they'd sort of like to know what became of him."

"Why not go to the police? They know more about the man than I do."

"Been there. The officer handling the enquiry is now off duty. And I don't want to be working when he comes on again. That will be at midnight."

"Oh well." It was evident from his attitude that the manager had already had more than his fill of the late occupant of apartment 824.

"If it's the right guy there's a reward," I hinted.

"Which you get."

"Sure. But I'd be prepared to spread say twenty-five dollars for all this cooperation I'm going to get around here."

He got up then, and took a key from a drawer.

"Nothing up there, but naturally if it'll help you."

The elevator shot smoothly to eight and we walked around a corner or two before reaching the apartment.

I thought apartment was a fairly toney word to be applied to the cramped room we entered. The manager was right. There was nothing here to tell me much about the recent tenant. He seemed to have been a neat, methodical kind of man, to judge by the contents of the drawers. His clothes were not expensive, but they were laundered and well cared for.

"Any family been around for that stuff?"

"No. You're the first one outside of the police."

I took a final look at the light gray suit hanging on the back of the door. It had nothing to tell me.

"What kind of looking man was he?"

The manager said suspiciously.

"If you're looking for a bond jumper, you have a full description. It's always circulated along with the wanted notice."

"Yes," I agreed patiently, "I know exactly what my man looks like. But I don't know whether this Brookman is my man."

That seemed to make sense. The manager scratched his head.

"Mind you, I never laid eyes on him personally. But various people here have described him so many times today that I have a kind of picture of him. I'd say he was over medium height, and on the thin side. That's being kind. At least two people have said he looked half-starved."

Three, I thought, if you counted Charlie Surprise. It began to sound like the same man.

"Did he have a job?"

"I doubt if he'd have had the time for any regular work. There were so many newspapers and books up here, all to do with horse-racing, I would say it must have taken all his time to keep up with them."

And that seemed to clinch it.

"You threw that stuff away?"

"Certainly not. I don't have the right. The rent is paid up to the end of the month. No, the police took it with them."

There wasn't much more to be learned there. I thanked the manager, promised to remember him if there was any reward due, and left.

It was the middle of the afternoon now, and the sun was quite fierce as I clambered back into the Chev. On a day like that a man should be down at the beach, loafing around and watching the maidens disport. Or else be sitting in some air-conditioned office where the sun would not be permitted to intrude. He ought not to be poking around crummy bars and seedy apartments making enquiries about a corpse. I ran a handkerchief around the inside of my collar for the second time, and started the motor.

It wasn't such a great distance physically from the Monterey Building to the Beach End, but at all other points of comparison they were miles apart. It took money, lots of money, to have a house at Beach End. It even took money to get the place in the first instance because competition is very fierce to acquire property up that way. I'd been there a time or two in the past, and it always left me with the same general feeling of dissatisfaction. I don't know why it should. I do all right out of my curious calling. In fact some people might think I was well off, but that is not the same thing as Beach End money. Out there, the favored residents have so much of the stuff they never even think about it any more.

Just to make things worse, the approach road runs parallel with the beach and I have to drive slowly to allow for the occasional beach ball that might come my way, hotly pursued by some bronzed slim female with shrieks of excitement. One such crossed my path, causing me to brake sharply. She was wearing two little pieces here and there which were not really worth the effort of putting them on. I sat waiting, grateful at least for the flashing smile which was to be my sole reward for saving her life. Might have got one too, except that some husky young blond bum came chasing after her, and with a few more shrieks she disappeared into some dunes on the far side of the road.

That didn't do either my imagination or my temper any good, and I was not feeling at my best when I arrived at the Somerset house. It was a white painted ranch style building with plenty of palm trees around. There was a huge heart-shaped swimming pool out front and that was when I remembered the house had one time belonged to Adele Ernest the movie queen. Still, that was no concern of mine. These days it belonged to one Hugo Somerset, entrepreneur. There were two cars in front, a week old Caddy, and a brand new M.G. It didn't seem fitting to park a three year old waggon next to such company, so I left it under some trees, telling myself it would be cooler there anyway.

My feet clumped on the verandah and I punched a silver bell which played the first two bars of Amour Amour. Nobody in the house seemed in the mood for amour, because I gave another chorus on the bell and still got no response. The door stood open and I could hear music faintly from inside.

Pushing the door wider I called out hallo, and nobody called back. I stepped inside, where it was cool and dim after the baking sun, and pointed my nose towards the music. It was coming from the back of the house, and soon I stood at the entrance to a large room. It was filled with divans and rugs, and at the far end was a bar. The bar was quite a feature, being made of black marble in the shape of a grand piano. There was one of those too, only this one was made of mahogany. A huge stereophonic record player dominated one wall and this was the source of the music, which was very relaxed and somehow soothing. I put it down as Tchaikovsky, because with all I know about music everything sounds like him. Not that I was concentrating too much on the music at that moment. I was busy staring at the man lying full length on one of the divans. He was huge, a great bull of a man with spare pink flesh hanging in folds from every part of him. He had a big, beefy face, ending in a ridiculous small ginger beard. Outside of the beard and his crop of red hair he was entirely naked, except for a small towel slung across where small towels ought to to be slung in such circumstances. He was looking at me, too, but without much interest.

"Excuse me——" I began.

He shook his fist angrily and pointed towards the cabinet. I was to shut up until the music finished. That was O.K. with me, so long as it didn't turn out to be one of these four hour concerts. Nobody invited me to make myself comfortable, so I perched on the edge of another divan, fishing around for an Old Favorite. The recumbent man snapped his fingers for one and I passed over the pack. He lifted a heavy silver lighter from the floor and lit the smoke, without offering to do anything about mine. Then he lay back again and closed his eyes.

I sat there thinking the fat man had the life, laying around in splendour. Listening to records and demanding cigarets from flunkeys while the rest of the world was out chasing its tail. The music lasted another fifteen minutes, then there was the gentlest of clicks and the machine switched itself out. For a moment I thought my silent companion would continue to ignore me, then he opened his eyes wide and looked at me.

"What did you think?"

"Beautiful," I admitted. Then plunging in, "Tchaikovsky, wasn't it?"

He looked at me to be certain I wasn't kidding. People are always doing that.

"Swan Lake," he rejoined. "Act Two. Notice anything?"

"Why er, no. Listen I'm not at all knowledgeable about music. About that kind of music," I amended.

"It's the sequence," he mused. "The musical sequences have been rearranged so as to permit logical following of the keys."

Despite my ignorance I couldn't help saying

"Don't you imagine the composer might prefer to have it played the way he wrote it down?"

He beat despairingly on his flabby chest with arms like logs.

"This is the way he wrote it down," he roared. "Other people have been monkeying with his original intentions for ninety years. Choreographers, dancers, musical directors, everybody. They didn't understand the man, he was ahead of his time."

It seemed that we were not talking so much about the music in its own right, as in its application to the ballet. I may not know a whole lot about classical music but when it comes to ballet I am the original man from Arkansas.

"Look, I know nothing about ballet——" I began.

But again he wasn't to be put off his stride.

"You know nothing about ballet," he sneered. "Of course you don't. Who do you think you are? There are people all over the world have spent their whole lives at it, and when Tchaikovsky's original score became available ten years back they mostly found they knew nothing about it either. I tell you there were some red faces around."

He wasn't trying to be offensive, I decided. It was just an effect he had on people.

"Could we talk about something else?" I suggested. "Like for instance what am I doing here?"

A great grin spread across his face, and now I realized what my memory had been searching for when I first saw him. He was the personification of those guys the old painters used to be so fond of. You know the ones, always sitting or lying around with an enormous goblet of the good juice in one hand, and a not over-modest lady in the other.

"Why, of course," he boomed. "What are you doing here?"

"I'm looking for a man named Hugo Somerset."

He sat up, scratching at the great pink belly.

"Your search is ended, my friend. Behold the man."

"The name is Preston. I'm a private investigator. Like to ask you a few questions about the man who died last night, Brookman."

"In that case we shall all need a drink," he decided. "Would you mind?"

He indicated the piano-shaped liquor cabinet. I went over there and opened it up. There were drinks in there even I had never heard of, and I've been around bars a long time.

"Make it something I can pronounce," I said.

He chuckled again.

"How about beer? You ought to be able to say that with a little practise."

I dug out a couple of frosted cans and tipped them carefully into tall tumblers which had not come free at the supermarket. I passed one to Somerset, and it disappeared inside the huge soft fist. The beer was very refreshing.

"You want to ask about Brookman? Well why not.

Everybody else in town has been treading all over the house all day. I like to think of myself as a democratic man. If somebody named Preston is of the opinion I should go through the whole circus again, why then you go right ahead."

I knew how he felt. Too often I get there after the police and the reporters.

"How well did you know him?"

"Not well at all. He's been around now for some months. Been to the house quite a bit."

"Do you always let people you don't know walk in and out of the house?"

"All the time," he returned equably. "Before we talk about Brookman it might be of help to you if we talk a little about me. Do you know anything about me?"

"Only what I read in the papers. They said you were an entrepreneur."

"That is so. Do you know what it means?"

"It's a Beach End word for promoter."

Again the booming laugh filled the room, and I watched with fascination the jiggling movements of various parts of the fat frame.

"That's neat. Maybe a little unkind, but not inaccurate. Yes, I think we could accept that. Somebody once said, those who can, do. Those who can't, teach. I'm one of those who can't, but I don't teach. As you quaintly put it, I promote."

"Promote what?"

"Anything artistic. Painters, poets, writers, musicians. If I find somebody who seems to have genuine talent, I sort of encourage them, foster them along. I am you see, tremendously artistic myself. Unfortunately, I haven't any talent, except for appreciation of what others do."

"That's a talent of its own," I offered. "And it must be a good feeling when you find someone."

His eyes lit up.

"Ah, there have been a few. Very few I'm afraid, but I have been right each time, and those people have gone on to do things."

"Could Brookman have been one of those?"

He shook his head emphatically.

"Not in a hundred years. He really did write poetry you know, and he assured me once that Poetry was his correct name. He did not manage to live up to that name. The kind of doggeral he churned out was no more than filth. Not suggestion executed with flair, there's sometimes room for that. Plain sewer muck."

Mr. Somerset evidently had not been impressed by Mr. Brookman's work.

"Then why have him around?"

"There you touch the sadness of my existence, Mr. Preston. My life is filled with Brookmans. Composers with no ear for music, writers who rehash an old Hemingway, singers who are tone deaf. If I'm lucky one of them may bring along a friend who really has something. Perhaps today, perhaps next year. It has happened before, it will happen again. But there are vast deserts in between."

"Is that damn music finished yet?"

I turned towards the new voice. A tall skinny brunette had come into the room. Her hair was drawn flat against her head and tied with a ribbon at the back. She had a thin, intense face, with large olive eyes which flashed with surprise as she saw me. She wasn't any more surprised than I was, because except for the ribbon she was completely naked. She showed no intention of leaving.

"Ah Flower, there you are."

"Who's the new chum?" she queried.

"This is a Mr. Preston," explained Somerset. "Mr. Preston is a detective."

"Not another one?" she sighed. "I thought you told me all those ghastly people had finished here."

She was leaning against the wall, for all the world as though it were a tea party. Since I was the only one who had any clothes on, I began to wonder whether it would seem more natural if I undressed too.

"This is Flower, Mr. Preston. One of my few comforts in this life, and as you can see, she can be quite a comfort."

I could see that all right. Her body was lean and smooth, with a tight flat stomach and small hard breasts. She was the same deep brown color all over, and it was evident that Flower didn't wear anything when she was outdoors in the sun, either. Under the circumstances it would have been ridiculous to say anything normal.

"You said she was one of your comforts. Could I see the others?"

The girl laughed, a surprisingly deep sound from that slim throat.

"You're not the ordinary run of flatfoot, are you?"

"I'm not with the force," I explained. "I'm private."

"You're here about Brookman, I imagine."

"Yes. But if I'm going to ask you any questions, I'll have to ask you to go away and put some clothes on first. My mind keeps coming up with the wrong questions."

Again came the deep laugh.

"Don't worry, I'm going. And never mind the questions. I can tell you all I know about the departed. He was a creep. Hugo, let me know when your nice friend leaves. Au revoir, Mr. Preston."

Despite her tough talk and unconventional dress habits, Flower had not started life on the wrong side of the tracks. I watched the slow rolling motion till she was out of sight.

"With your permission Mr. Somerset," I said formally. "I could do with another drink."

35

"Help yourself. Aren't you going to ask me about Flower?"

I broke open the can and refilled my glass.

"None of my business, is it? I find if people want me to know things, they'll tell me."

He stared at me hard, something like amusement in his eyes.

"She was right, you are no ordinary flatfoot. Very well, shall we talk about Brookman?"

"That's why I came. How long did you know him?"

"I was trying to remember that for the police. One can't be too exact with such a casual acquaintance. I'd say between three and six months."

"Did he do any kind of work?"

"Not to my knowledge. He was always borrowing money. And of course, he never sold a verse in his life."

I tipped some more of the cold beer down my throat.

"When he came here was he alone, or with some special people?"

"Mostly alone, I believe. Of course he knew a lot of the crowd to say hallo to, either from meeting them here or at the Speckled Band. Sorry, you may not know where that is?"

I nodded sadly.

"I know where it is all right. I had to go there one time. To be certain I got in I had to dress up like something got washed up on the beach."

The big man inclined his head gravely.

"It does have some odd associations," he admitted. "However it's like this house, full of people from a maniac's nightmare, one of whom could turn out to be a genius."

It seemed like an awful hard way to find a genius. Personally I'd as soon file a notice in the Genius Wanted columns.

"One last thing, Mr. Somerset. Was there anything special about the night of the party?"

"There is always something special about my parties," he said loftily.

"But if you mean anything connected with Brookman, the answer is no."

And it was clearly implied by his tone that the something special which had nothing to do with Brookman, had nothing to do with me either.

"Well thanks, Mr. Somerset, you've been very obliging. I won't take up any more of your time. If anything should come to mind, I'd certainly appreciate it if you'd give me a call."

He looked at the little white card I handed over.

"Parkside Towers," he mused. "You must either be a very good detective or you have some other source of income. I believe the rental over there is rather out of the coffee and cakes level."

"It's robbery," I assured him. "And you're beginning to sound like the Bureau of Inland Revenue. Let's say I'm lucky." He let me hear the rich chuckle just one more time. Hugo Somerset might be an oddball, alright he was an oddball but there was something about the man I couldn't help liking. I thanked him for the beer, and he waved a flabby arm as I left.

When I stepped through the front door of the house, there was Flower. She was sprawled out in a long basket-work chair, carefully covered in a black and yellow silk Japanese kimono. Perversely, I now found her much more attractive than when she'd been wearing all that skin.

"You ought to get dressed more often," I told her. "On you clothes look good."

She smiled slowly up at me, even white teeth flashing against the browny red lips. It was the smile of a woman who'd smiled before, plenty of other times, plenty of other places. And not always outside in a garden.

"Hugo wouldn't tell you anything, would he?"

"He told me what he could."

"I could tell you more," she coaxed.

"So tell me."

She held up her arms, and sighed.

"Come and be nice to me, and perhaps I will."

There was a fleeting moment when I almost did. With an effort I made myself realize how ridiculous a situation it was.

"Lady, it would be a privilege. But right now I'm very hot, the circumstances are very slightly unsuitable, and it seems to me the heat must be making you very slightly daffy. What about Brookman?"

She folded her arms across the flat stomach, and pouted like a child.

"Shan't tell you. How can you be so pretty and so horrible all at the same time?"

"How can you be so beautiful and such a screwball?" I countered. "You realize we could be seen from the public highway. It may give you some kind of kick to appear on a flagrant indecency rap, but include me out. Tell me about Brookman."

She ran a small pink tongue across her lips and pondered.

"Not now," she decided finally. "Maybe one day, but not now."

"Suit yourself. If you ever feel talkative, you'll find my number in the book."

"There's lots of Prestons in there. What kind of Preston would you be?"

38

"Kind of a Mark Preston."

"Mark Preston. Nice. So long Mark Preston. You'd better go, or you'll be late for Sunday school."

I could feel her mocking eyes on my back all the way down the drive.

CHAPTER FOUR

As I drove back the sun was half-way towards the horizon, striking a million sparkles from the deep blue of the water. On the white sands the beach crowd had mostly had enough of the swimming and ball games for today. Instead they were lazing around, reading, sipping at iced drinks. The younger ones were showing the early signs of turning their attentions to other things, things which hadn't any connection with beach ball. I drove slowly, soaking up the relaxed atmosphere. From such surroundings, there could be all kinds of places I could logically be heading for. Naturally, I went to the morgue. The attendant knew me, and that struck a hollow note. After all, how many people can reasonably expect to be remembered on sight by mortuary attendants?

"Hi, Mr. Preston. Hot ain't it?"

"Hallo, Sid. You had a customer today. Guy who fell off Indian Point."

"Sure. He's in twenty-six. You wanta see him?"

No, I did not want to see him. But I knew I had to. My unwilling feet dragged along the stone passage after Sid.

"This here's the guy."

He grabbed a handle and pulled out the drawer-like refrigerated slab. I took my one and only look at Mr. Poetry Brookman, poet, aged 31. The front of his face wasn't too badly damaged at all, and I was fairly satisfied this was the man I'd been hearing described all afternoon.

"Don't look too bad now, does he?" queried Sid. "I

40

tell you, these young docs these days, they do a marvellous job. Of course, they couldn't do a lot with the back of his head. You wanta see?"

I shook my head and walked back outside. Sid came along after me.

"Want you to do something for me, Sid."

"Any time Mr. Preston. You know that."

"First, don't tell the police I was here."

He screwed up his mouth dolefully.

"You know I have to tell them. Part of my job."

I held out two tens, and he looked at them with interest.

"Is it that much a part of your job?"

He shook his head stubbornly.

"Like to help you Mr. Preston. And that twenty looks good. But I ain't chancing my job, and my pension and everything for twenty bucks."

And I could tell it wouldn't do any good to increase it either.

"If that's how you feel," I shrugged. "At least don't tell them I asked you not to."

"Sure not. You don't imagine I'm here to get people in trouble?"

"No. All right, here's something you can do. Let me know about anyone who asks to see the body. Excluding policemen and newspaper reporters, that is."

He thought about it for a moment.

"Doesn't sound to be no harm in that," he said dubiously.

"There isn't," I assured him. "After all, if I care to park outside the front entrance all day, I'd see for myself, wouldn't I? All I'm asking you to do is save me from getting baked to death in a car."

"Yeah. That's true, you could do that. O.K. Mr. Preston, guess this makes me kind of a special agent, huh?"

"Something like that. I'll see if I can get you a ranger badge."

He took the twenty this time.

"It just so happens I can produce some results right off the cuff. Come into the office."

We went into the partitioned square which he dignified under the description of office, and he rifled importantly at a small tray of white cards.

"Here it is. She was here this afternoon, two o'clock, two-thirty."

I wrote down "Mrs. Evelyn Prince" and an address way over on the Heights. A man has to be lucky sometimes, the place was less than a mile from Parkside Towers.

"Don't think it'll do you any good, mind," warned Sid.

"How come?"

"She didn't know him. The reason she came, she thought it could be a relative. Seems this relative went missing one time, and from the description in the paper this Brookman could be the guy. So she just came to check. When she saw the body, she was so happy it was the wrong man she bust out crying right there. I was glad, too."

That didn't sound like Sid. He didn't usually enjoy watching people suffer.

"You were glad she cried?" I asked stiffly.

"Nah. I mean I was glad it wasn't no relative. She was a lady, a real nice lady. She shouldn't have no business with relatives like that bum in there. She can't help you."

"Well, thanks for saving me a trip."

I crumpled up the note I'd made and dropped it in the waste bin. Sid nodded with approval. A lady who didn't have bum relatives had no business being chivvied around by bum private investigators either.

"But if anyone else looks in, you'll call me, huh?"

"Bet."

I went back and sat in the car thinking. Then I drove out to the Heights. The Prince house lay back from the road in a tree-lined avenue. It wasn't Beach End property, but nevertheless way up in the middle income group. I had a feeling somebody was watching me as I walked up the flagged path between neat lawns. I was right too because the door opened before I had a chance to knock. A tall gangling boy leaned in the doorway inspecting me. He was about fifteen years old, with a check shirt and battered jeans covering the skinny frame.

"Well?" he demanded insolently.

He was one of those people I could learn to dislike fast.

"I'd like to see Mrs. Evelyn Prince," I told him.

"What about?"

He showed no sign of interest in the answer, eyes looking over my shoulder into the road, in case anything more interesting should happen along.

"I'll discuss it with her, if you don't mind."

"I do mind. You could be some kind of nut or something. You could be just going around cutting up women or like that. A guy has a right to protect his mother."

"All right little man," I sighed. "Here."

I flashed my license just long enough for him to read the part which said boldly "State of California," without giving him time to get down to the details.

He sneered.

"Fuzz, huh? Well, you better come in. Leave us not keep the guardians of the peace standing out in the rain."

He took me into a pleasant room overlooking a secluded garden.

"You wait here and I'll tell her. You don't want to tell me what it is she's done, I guess?"

From the way he spoke, he wouldn't have cared too much if his mother was a multiple murderer.

"Just tell her."

He went away and I looked round the room. It was the kind of place I didn't get to see often enough. A room for family life, sitting around talking or reading. A place where people lived, people who had no business with characters who got shot in the head and pushed off cliffs. There were bookshelves along one wall and I studied these idly. Mostly novels, and soft cover reprints, there was one section which made me take a second look. Each book in the section had to do with something artistic. I saw Shelley and a History of the Bolshoi, something about Rembrandt, when a voice said

"You wished to see me?"

I turned at once, and looked at the woman who had come in. She could be in her late thirties at a guess, tall and dark. Her figure was full and not yet run to seed, the discreet green afternoon dress doing little to conceal the almost aggressive femininity. She had a strong handsome face, with far too much character in it to be described as beautiful. She had been crying too, despite the fresh make-up around her puffy eyes. Behind her, the boy lounged, waiting to see what went on.

"Mrs. Prince," I assumed. "This won't take long. If I could see you alone?"

I nodded towards the kid, who scowled. His mother turned to him.

"Harry, go and find something to do."

"I don't think I ought. For all we know this guy might start laying into you with a rubber hose. I know all about their dirty little ways."

"That will do, Harry," snapped his mother. "Now do as I say."

To my surprise the boy, after one last insolent shrug,

turned and slouched out of the house, slamming the front door.

"You mustn't mind Harry. He watches too much television," she smiled. "Please sit down Mr.——"

"Preston. Thank you."

We sat down, Mrs. Prince arranging her skirt demurely, so that I didn't see more than I should of the long splendid legs.

"Well now," she began brightly, "It can't be a motoring offense. You always send a uniformed officer for those."

She was uncertain, for some reason. A suburban matron, right in her own backyard, disturbed, but quite determined that nothing would be permitted to interrupt the domestic routine. Whatever it was I wanted, rape, arson, burglary, she would help if possible of course. But I would appreciate I must be gone, like the daily help, by cocktail time. The universal female.

"No ma'am, it has nothing to do with cars. It's something rather more serious. You're quite sure your son won't be able to overhear?"

She smiled briefly.

"You mean Mr. Preston, am I quite sure he won't eavesdrop. Well, I never met a child who wouldn't. That's why I sent him out of the house. He can't get back in without my hearing. We're quite safe."

I thought the description child was rather inadequate for close to six feet of potential, if not actual, delinquent. But I hadn't come about Harry. To my surprise, she continued speaking.

"You see it's terribly difficult now that he's getting older. A boy that size needs a father. Of course I work extra hard with him, but a woman alone is not always an adequate substitute." She watched anxiously for my response, and that was the first time it dawned on me. She wasn't concerned for herself at all. She thought darling

Harry had probably stuck up a cigar store, or kidnapped a baby or something. Having seen him, I could understand her concern.

"I quite see that Mrs. Prince," I assured her. "And if you're thinking my visit has something to do with your son, please put your mind at rest. I've never heard a word said against him."

Which was perfectly true.

Gratitude and relief fought for supremacy on her face.

"You must think I'm awfully silly, jumping to conclusions."

"Very understandable. But I'm here about something quite different."

I was beginning to wish I'd followed Sid's advice. Here I was, getting a mother all worked up over her son, letting her off the hook, then preparing to slam another one in while she was still on the line.

"I'm making enquiries about a man who was murdered last night. I have information that you knew the man."

Her face set back into tight lines, and each word was inspected carefully before issue.

"What could I possibly know about such people?"

"How do you mean, 'such people'?" I queried.

She flushed, and spoke more quickly.

"I meant people who get mixed up in that kind of thing. It may be a matter of daily routine for you Mr. Preston, but this is hardly the kind of neighborhood in which we have any contact with those things. I don't see how I can possibly help you."

This wasn't a worried mother any longer. Now that the young were in a place of safety, the female of the species was back to her more accustomed role. Now she was herself, calm, resourceful, watchful.

"Maybe you don't read the newspapers Mrs. Prince," I

told her. "Murder is no great respecter of persons, or property. I find myself asking questions at addresses like this just as often as I do down Conquest Street. And it is less than two years since a woman a block from here shot her husband, in case you'd forgotten it."

But her self-assurance was all around her now like a steel wall.

"I'm sure you must have many interesting stories to tell," she said bitingly. "However, to save you the trouble, I ought to tell you I majored in sociology."

I'd have to try something more direct.

"Mrs. Prince. we could go on like this all day. When I came here, I had strong doubts whether you could tell me anything which would help very much. By being deliberately evasive, you're beginning to make me wonder."

"I can scarcely be responsible for what you think."

I set my face into lines of disapproval.

"So you refuse to tell me what you know?"

"Not at all," she was quite unflustered. "It is simply that I don't have anything to tell you."

"And you never heard of a man named Brookman?" I pressed.

That was when she overdid it.

"Brookman?" she puzzled. "No, I don't believe so. What does he do?"

"He doesn't do anything," I informed her. "Except lie around on a slab in the city mortuary. If you'll forgive my mentioning such things in this lovely neighborhood."

She stood up and walked to the door.

"This is my house, and we don't have a police state. You can't force your way in and bully people like this."

I got up and made a half-bow.

"I was invited in," I reminded her. "And I was only

following up a routine enquiry. If you'd cooperated, you would have been rid of me in five minutes. Now, we'll have to start to dig. I don't know what we'll come up with, but clearly there's something to be found."

I walked past her to the street door.

"Mr. Preston."

She had followed me, and now placed a hand on my arm.

"Yes?"

"Please come back."

So there we were again, sitting looking at each other. But this time her hands were pressed tightly together over her knees.

"What is it you want to know?"

"I've no idea," I said flatly. "Just anything you happen to know about this, which may or may not be useful."

She nodded absently, staring beyond me to the book-lined wall. When she spoke, her voice was far away.

"Life can be very lonely for a woman with no husband. She has to develop interests, things which will get her out of the house. Without them, she'd spend all her time alone. When she lets that happen, she may as well shrivel up and die." That didn't seem to call for much comment from me. I avoided her eyes and waited.

"But, on the other hand," she continued, "Such a woman has also to be very careful about her activities. She is a natural readymade subject for scandal. I can't afford to run the least risk with my reputation, Mr. Preston. I have a position to maintain here, and a son to consider."

She had suddenly switched from the abstract lecture and started talking about herself.

"There's always somebody with a nasty tongue." I replied sympathetically.

There was a quick grateful look on her face.

"I try to find interests where there are a number of other people concerned, so that I'm always merely one of a crowd. I feel it makes me less vulnerable. Play readings, organised tours, things of that nature. That was how I became involved with that man."

"I see. What were the circumstances, Mrs. Prince?"

She got up and went to the window. She was probably hoping that when she looked round I'd be gone. I wasn't.

"I was invited to a private recital, a piano recital. There was this young man who was rumoured to be another Paderewski. I am interested in anything like that, so I went. I didn't much like the look of some of the people there when I arrived, but I couldn't see that it mattered very much. After all, we were all there to listen. Well, we had this so-called recital. The brilliant soloist turned out to be a barely adequate performer, and had it not been a private affair, quite frankly I would have walked out. Since then, I've always regretted not doing so."

She paced up and down a couple of times, then came and sat down again.

"Mr. Preston, this is terribly difficult for me. I suppose—I suppose you have to make out a report about everything?"

I shook my head.

"Not at all. The only things I'm interested in are those which have a direct bearing on this murder. The rest I forget."

She nodded uncertainly, as though anxious to believe me, but finding it difficult.

"I see. Well, as you may know, the usual thing after an event of this kind is for everyone to stay on for a while. There may be a glass of sherry and a sandwich perhaps, and everyone discusses the performance. I expected something of the kind to happen. I can scarcely bring myself to remember what really happened."

"Things got a little out of hand?" I suggested tact-fully.

She laughed briefly and bitterly.

"I'm not going into any details. Everyone seemed to go mad. It was like one of those old Roman orgies one reads about. Some man, I'd never even seen him before, started to. . . ." her voice trailed away. Then she gritted her teeth and inspected the floor. Each word now was uttered slowly and distinctly. "This man began to un-dress me. I was so shocked and frightened, I lost control of myself. I kicked him, punched him, heaven knows he didn't seem at all put off by my reaction. In fact he quite obviously enjoyed it. Nobody else in the place, there must have been twenty or twenty-five people there, none of them took the slightest notice. I don't remember when I've been so frightened."

She broke off for a moment, and there was an uncom-fortable silence. I sat absolutely wooden, because Eve Prince was wound up tight, and the slightest distraction from me might cause her to break down.

"The man was wearing me down," she resumed "And then another man came up and spoke to him. I don't know what he said, but it was certainly effective. The big one just let go of me and walked away. He didn't even argue. This new man told me I had no business to be there. He advised me to get out there and then, and believe me I didn't need to be told. I tried to thank him, but he wasn't interested. He walked me to the door, made me promise I would say nothing to anyone about what had happened. I'd have promised anybody anything to be free of that terrible place."

The worst part was over now, and it was safe for me to speak.

"You were very lucky to get away like that." I pointed out.

"Yes. I started out immediately for the police, but of course I never got there. As soon as I was calm enough to think properly, I could foresee that if I did that, my future in Monkton City was finished. I would always be the woman who went to vice parties, no matter what the circumstances were."

"Not at all," I objected. "Your name would never have been mentioned at any trial. You would have been Mrs. X."

I didn't sound very convincing though, for the reason that I didn't believe it myself. Even if the decent newspapers decided to give her a break, there'd be some dirt-hunting hack who'd come up with a picture of the "lovely Mrs. X, mysterious orgy witness," and after that Eve Prince might as well leave town.

"I'm sure you don't have any more faith in that than I," she reproved. "Anyway, I didn't report it. Next morning I made the acquaintance of this man Brookman. He telephoned the house and told me he was going to call to discuss the party the previous night. I need hardly describe my feelings while I waited for him. I was afraid to have him in the house, so I waited out front. When he came, he had some photographs. They were all of me, and they were all very clear. He said he'd been of great service to me, because the man who took the pictures wanted five hundred dollars for them. Brookman had persuaded him to accept two hundred. I paid of course."

"And how often did he turn up after that?"

"Every two weeks. It's been going on almost three months now."

Three months of blackmail at that cost would probably have begun to put a real strain on her resources, I would guess.

"And now he's dead," I mused. "You realize, Mrs. Prince, that I have to take a special interest in you now?"

51

She looked surprised.

"I don't see why," she objected. "I've told you the whole thing."

"What you have told me," I explained, "Is a good sound reason for wanting Brookman dead. He is dead, and it would have been an entirely understandable thing if you'd been the one to kill him."

"Oh."

She made a tight little sound and bit anxiously at her knuckles.

"Mr. Preston, I had nothing to do with it. When I read the story in the newspaper I could hardly believe it. I went to the mortuary to see for myself whether it was the right man."

And that was that, so far as she could see. The world is not that easy to live in.

"Where were you last night?"

"I was here at home," she said icily. "And, oh yes, I can prove it. My son had a couple of his friends in here and they were playing records until quite late."

"That's very good news Mrs. Prince. And I'm very interested in hearing about Brookman's blackmail activities. If he had any other—er—victims. I ought to have some very profitable enquiries to make. I think a good place to start would be wherever this phoney piano recital was held."

I raised my voice at the end to make it a question. She was alarmed at once.

"But I don't want any more involvement," she protested. "It was a filthy incident, a nasty ugly hour in my life that I just want to forget, I won't testify, you know."

She said that bit triumphantly as though it were a trump card.

"Nobody said anything about testimony," I pointed out wearily.

"All I want is to contact these people who obviously must have known Brookman. This is a very elusive guy so far as his private life is concerned. No family, no friends I can trace. All I'm asking is the address. Your name won't be mentioned."

"If I thought I could rely on that——" she hesitated.

"You can," I promised.

"Very well. It's a house out at Beach End. I've forgotten the name of the house, but it belongs to a man named Hugo Somerset."

I should have been able to guess that.

"You know this Somerset?"

"No. But he was there, acting as a combined host and master of ceremonies."

I paused before asking the next question. But it had to be asked.

"Eer, this Hugo Somerset. It wasn't him who er— er——"

She shook her head hard.

"No, it wasn't him. He was the one who put a stop to it."

One of the Santa Claus Somersets, I reflected.

"Well, I guess I can get the address easily enough. Thank you, Mrs. Prince. I'm sorry you've been bothered about all this, and I can understand the way you feel. There's just one last thing."

She looked up at me as I stood, and worry or not on her face, she was a very attractive woman.

"Yes?"

"Blackmailers sometimes have friends. Either that, or somebody else who finds the blackmail material. Such a person might decide it would be a good idea to carry on where Brookman left off."

I wasn't doing a whole lot to help her lose that worried expression.

"I had thought of that," she admitted.

"Right. Now if any such thing should happen, if anybody else tries to blackmail you, I want you to promise to get in touch with me."

I scribbled my apartment phone number on a piece of paper and handed it to her.

"But if I do that, I'm no better off than before. The whole thing will come out," she wailed.

"No, no," I soothed, and I meant it. "It won't come out. I'll just have a private talk with whoever it is, and you'll hear no more."

She was anxious to be convinced but I wasn't satisfied she'd do as I asked.

"Remember," I added solemnly. "Whoever calls you, if anyone does, could be Brookman's murderer. You wouldn't want to take a chance with anybody like that."

She nodded dejectedly.

"You're right of course. And I will telephone."

"Thank you."

She watched me walk down to the car. I gave her a small wave as I drove away but she didn't respond. It seemed to be my day for walking away from beautiful women.

CHAPTER FIVE

My stomach kept muttering about people with irregular eating habits, so I stopped over at a small Austrian place and helped myself to a portion of the gefillte fish. Along with this I washed down a glass or two of a special dry white wine they serve in there. I'm a great believer in keeping the eating varied. Sometimes it's Chinese food, sometimes Italian, now and then I go kosher. But it seems wherever I go I can't get away from people.

"Whatever happened to that big fat story I was going to get?"

I looked up as Shad Steiner pulled out the chair opposite and sat down.

"Join me," I suggested.

"I already did. No story, huh?"

"I'm working on it. You going to eat?"

"I finished ten minutes ago. But thanks, I'll join you in the wine. Hey waiter, another glass here."

I watched sadly as he tipped most of the remaining contents of the bottle down his throat.

"That's wine you know, not lemonade," I told him bitterly.

He shrugged his shoulders and put down the glass.

"Don't tell me about wine, please. My father worked in the vineyards all his life in the old country. I forgot more about wine by the time I'm ten years old than you'll learn in your whole life. And don't change the subject."

"There's nothing to talk about yet," I said.

"There isn't going to be, if you spend your whole life in wine shops. You ought to be out and around."

"Out and around I have been. This is my first food today. Tell me, what's the dirt on this Hugo Somerset?"

He thoughtfully shared out the remaining wine between us. One inch in my glass, three in his.

"Why would there be any?" he demanded.

"I had a talk with him today. An oddball, to say the least, and as you told me this morning, he sure knows some funny people. I thought there may be something else you know about him, I mean before this Brookman thing. He seems to have a lot of money, for instance. Where does it come from?"

Steiner peered at me across the table, the wise old face threaded with lines of suspicion.

"The guy is somewhat of a mystery," he admitted grudgingly. "He doesn't seem to have been born anywhere. He turns up here in Monkton about six years ago, a full-grown man. He sets up at the Beach End and starts living like money. If he has any business interests they're certainly not in this town."

"And he hasn't been in any police trouble? No dames, no drunk parties?"

The newspaperman smiled and shook his head.

"Drunk parties?" he echoed. "People at Beach End don't have drunk parties. They have a few friends in for cocktails. Or an evening of celebration. How many times do you read in the Globe about the honorable mister who'sit entertaining friends last night? It happens all the time. But drunk parties, uh uh. Such descriptions are not for Beach End wingdings."

"How about all this artistic stuff? Did he ever really turn up somebody with talent?"

Steiner grinned knowingly and tapped at his nose with a bony forefinger.

"You have an odd habit of coming up with the same questions I do myself. But hours later, naturally."

"Naturally. How about the answer?"

"I asked my Art Editor the same thing this morning. He couldn't be certain off hand so he had the files checked. The answer, as they say, is in the affirmative. Mr. Somerset has delivered on about four occasions over the years. Unknowns that he seems to have found and promoted, all of them now well settled in their different fields."

And that would agree with the way Somerset had talked to me that afternoon. In a way I was disappointed. I'd been hoping vaguely the whole bit was a huge con, nothing more than a cover for an elaborate blackmail network.

"Do you know whether the police had made any progress today?" I asked.

"I don't think so. I've had one man spend a little time on it, and he didn't come up with anything. After all it's just a two-bit killing, nothing for any of us to get worked up about. When you consider the homicide turnover in this fair city, nobody has too much time to spare on a no-hoper like Brookman. Tonight, or maybe tomorrow, we'll have a nice love-nest butchery, or something with some meat on it, then we can all forget about Brookman."

He was right of course. In a way he was echoing what Jake Martello had said earlier. Neither police nor newspapers had enough time or resources to dig too deeply into a backyard affair like the Brookman killing. And it would look suspicious if I seemed too interested.

"You're right Shad. I don't think I'll waste a lot more time on it myself. If I don't come up with anything pretty fast, I'll have to look for something more profitable."

He nodded, but whether to indicate he agreed with me

57

or not, I couldn't tell. With Steiner, I never could tell.

We left the restaurant together, and he refused a lift, walking briskly away on the fifteen minute hike back to his home. I got in the Chev and went back to Parkside. After the heat of the day I thought I was entitled to a shower before the night shift. As I got out of the car I noticed a plain police sedan parked just ahead. I walked towards the entrance, and at the same time a man climbed out of the police waggon and headed for me. It was Randall, sergeant from Homicide and Lieutenant Rourke's right hand man.

"Lo Preston, been waiting for you."

I turned to look at him. Randall is a big man. He's as tall as me, a little over six feet, and half as wide again. It makes him look heavy and ponderous. He isn't. He has a large fleshy face, with deep-set eyes threatened with engulfment by the heavy surrounding folds of flesh. These make him look half-asleep. He isn't. Looking at him, you could easily get the impression of a man lumbering around the world, a man not too strong on intelligence. And you would be getting a very wrong impression indeed.

"Hi, Gil. Collecting for the Benefit Fund?"

"Not this trip. Do I come up?"

"Why not?"

We went up in silence. I wondered vaguely what he was after, but I wasn't too concerned. It was one of those infrequent periods of my life when I wasn't doing anything I wouldn't want the police to know about. On the other hand, it was unlikely to be a social visit. Randall wasn't in the habit of making those. Not to me anyway.

We went into the apartment, and I flicked on some light. Randall sighed, looking around.

"This place always irritates me."

"Why, what's wrong with it?"

His face contorted into a scowl.

"Nothing's wrong with it, that's what's wrong with it. There isn't a cop on the force, including the commissioner, can afford anything like this. How do you rate it, if you do honest work?"

"My clients seem to be more generous than the taxpayers," I told him.

"That they do. Maybe we should ask the Bureau to look into your income tax situation."

He wasn't picking on me in particular. It was no more than the normal bitterness of an honest policeman, required to work all hours of the day and night, to be beaten up or shot at in alleyways, all for less pay than the grateful public would pay a waiter.

"The books are available in my office at all times. You can call in the Bureau, the Treasury men, anybody you like. Those books are in order. And there's just the one set, incidentally."

He snorted and stretched himself out in one of my best chairs.

"Seems to me in a swank place like this a man could get himself a cold beer," he grumbled.

I went and broke out a couple of cans and we sat opposite each other, sipping.

"Now that we've exhausted the income tax position," I said, "Was there anything else?"

He shrugged the massive shoulders.

"Nothing important, I hardly like to bother you."

When Randall says it isn't important, it usually means somebody is in a lot of trouble. And the somebody was going to be me.

"O.K. Well then let's forget it," I suggested. "I have a pretty tight schedule tonight anyway."

"Naw, it'll only take a minute. It's a little matter of——"

The phone shrilled, and he broke off in mid-sentence. I looked at him, waiting for him to finish.

"Aren't you going to answer that?" he queried. "If I'm lucky it could be something illegal and I could put the arm on you straight away."

"Thanks."

I went across and picked up the receiver.

"Preston."

"Listen, this is Flower."

Her voice was low and anxious, as though afraid someone might overhear.

"What can I do for you?" I said guardedly.

"I have to see you, right away, now."

"What about?"

"Please," she begged, and there was no missing the sincerity in her voice, "Please, you have to come."

"I can't," I hedged. "I have company."

"Well get rid of her," she whispered. "I'll see to it that you don't regret it, whoever she is."

"It's not a she, it's a he. All right, if it's so important, I could probably make it, in say half an hour. Where?"

"Come to Brookman's apartment. You know where it is?"

"Yes," I replied slowly, "I know it. But I don't get any of this."

"You will. Half an hour. You promise?"

"I promise."

I cradled the receiver and went back to my chair. I didn't want to talk to Randall. I wanted to see Flower, and find out what her connection was with Brookman's apartment, and what was so important that she had to tell me, and who it was at the other end wasn't supposed to know about the call.

"Yup, this is the life," intoned Randall. "Sitting around

in a swell apartment, swilling cold beer on a warm evening, just waiting for the dames to call up."

"This is a slack time," I assured him. "Normally I have three or four of them sitting around, waiting for me to choose."

"Yes," he sighed. "You're going to miss all this."

"How am I going to miss it?" I demanded. "Am I going somewhere?"

"Could be."

He finished the last of the beer and smacked his lips.

"Preston, you have been around now how long?"

"Too long."

"Right. I never can make out just what it is you do keeps you living it up this way. But whatever, you been doing it a long time. You know the score, and most of the time you have enough sense to keep out of the department's hair. In an off-beat kind of way, we practically trust you."

The words themselves were scarcely flattering, but coming from Gil Randall they amounted to an illuminated scroll.

"I try to get along with you guys," I said carefully.

"That's what we like to think down at headquarters. So what makes you pull a bum stunt like this afternoon?"

A typical Randall manouver. He left it for me to supply the details.

"I pulled a lot of bum stunts today," I told him. "You wouldn't want me to go and admit to one you don't know about yet."

"All right," he held up a weary hand. "I'll spell it out for you. You've been impersonating a police officer."

Eve Prince. I'd bluffed the boy, Harry, by not letting him get a proper look at my sticker. But she couldn't have complained. After telling me what she had, she'd be too afraid I'd repeat it.

"Did I do that today? Was that the time I conned this old lady out of her life savings?"

The deep eyes were little more than slits.

"You were always fast with the words. There was this telephone call to headquarters. Woman asking for Detective Preston."

"So who says that was me?" I asked in an injured tone.

"She does. So do we. What do you say?"

"I don't say anything till I hear more about it. This has all the earmarks of a set-up."

It was the wrong word. Angrily, Randall spat.

"Don't you talk to me about set-ups, Preston. This is a big town with a clean department and I have a lot of years behind me on this job. So don't talk to me about set-ups. When we take people in we take 'em good, and we don't need any phoney tricks to do it. You can be in a lotta trouble right here, and if you don't talk polite I'll make personally certain you get every last bit of it. Am I getting through to you?"

"Got it. But I still don't know what it's all about."

I had this feeling that Randall wasn't too sure of his ground. If he really knew what he was about, he'd have grabbed me the moment he saw me downstairs. And he wouldn't have sat around drinking my beer, he's not that kind of cop. Now he watched my face.

"You want it in pieces, I'll give it you. You called on a Mrs. Prince this afternoon, I have the address here."

He began digging in his pocket, but I waved him down.

"No need, I know the address. Sure, I was there. What about it?"

"You admit it, that's good. That saves procedure. You told this woman you were a police officer and——"

"No," I denied flatly.

"She says you did."

"I don't believe she said that either."

He corrugated his brows in a rugged frown.

"You calling me a liar, Preston?"

"I'm saying there's some confusion here. I called on this woman and talked with her. At no time did I say I was a police officer, and if she said anything of the kind to you I'd be very much surprised."

Randall chewed carefully at the inside of his jaw and didn't take his eyes off my face while he digested that one.

"You deny it, huh?"

"One hundred per cent. And if you're going to pinch me on a defended charge like this, you have to have a witness for the prosecution. And I'm saying Mrs. Prince would never be that witness. There's something mixed up here."

"Don't try to teach me the law," he snapped, "I know a little odd piece of it here and there myself. A mix-up you say?"

"That's what I say. And you know me better than to imagine I'd be such a fool. This is not my first day on the job, you know."

"H'm."

He got up and prowled around the room.

"Nice place. What did you talk about?"

I laughed and sat back in the chair.

"Come on, you know I'm not going to tell you that."

"Suppose I ask her?"

"Help yourself."

He stood to one side, looking at me carefully for a full minute. Then he walked to the door.

"I may do that. Maybe there is a mix-up. But if it sticks, don't make any appointments for the next year or so."

He went out quietly, and I gave a huge sigh of relief.

Checking my watch I found I had fifteen minutes to keep my date with Flower. But first I had to call Eve Prince, otherwise I'd have a date with a small gray room. She answered on the second ring.

"Mrs. Prince? This is Preston."

"Oh."

She didn't sound exactly overjoyed.

"Look, we seem to have had a little misunderstanding, so I thought I should phone and straighten it out."

"I don't think so," she replied bitterly. "I don't think there's any misunderstanding whatever. You came here under false pretenses, wormed a rather sordid story out of me, and now we come to the part where I pay you instead of Brookman. Would that be correct?"

Her voice was faraway, almost sing-song. I realized that to her it might seem the nightmare had started over. As gently as I could I said,

"Now Mrs. Prince, please be calm and believe what I'm telling you. I'm a fully licensed private investigator. That is to say I am licensed by the State of California as well as by the local city authorities. Believe me, I am very well known in this city. Do you have a lawyer friend or do you happen to know a judge, or a senior police officer?"

"I have my own lawyer," she said doubtfully.

"All right, fine. Now don't take my word for this. As soon as we've talked, you call him, ask him about me. The chances are, he'll know himself, but if so happens he doesn't he can check me out in five minutes flat. Now, will you do that please?"

There was a pause at the other end while she worried at it.

"It certainly sounds all right," she said dubiously.

"It is all right. And it's essential you feel satisfied about me, because we could both be in trouble."

"Both?" she didn't like the sound of that.

"Yes. Now listen carefully. The police have been to see me. According to them, you have reported that I've been impersonating a police officer. Is that true?"

Another pause.

"No. Or rather, in a way, I suppose."

"In what way, Mrs. Prince?"

"Look, you remember you gave me your telephone number?"

"Yes."

"I was to call you if I thought of anything. Well something came to me, and I rang you. When I didn't get any answer, I called police headquarters and asked for you there. They said they didn't have a Detective Preston, and started asking all kinds of questions. I—I just hung up on them."

So that was it. And of course they would have taken her name and address the moment they answered the phone. That was routine procedure.

"So you didn't actually tell cnem anything?"

"No, I sort of panicked. All I could think was that the whole thing would come out in the open, and I lost my head. I simply put down the telephone."

I thought rapidly.

"If that's all that happened, I don't think we need worry. Now listen very carefully. You may be called on, but don't be afraid. You simply have to say you made a mistake. You can say you knew perfectly well I was a private detective. You can say I made that very clear to you."

"Then why did I call them?" she wanted to know.

"Can you put on some kind of an act? Can you pretend you don't know very much about these things and you thought private detectives were policemen who didn't wear uniforms?"

"It doesn't make me sound very intelligent," she said without enthusiasm.

"Maybe not. But it's the kind of nutty thing the police are used to. They get this kind of thinking a dozen times a day from the public. If you act a little bit scatterbrained, you know, silly old me, the officer will not be remotely surprised. Half their time is spent on following up useless enquiries. Do you think you can do that?"

"Yes. Yes I can."

She still didn't sound too convinced, but I'd just have to leave her to do her best now.

"And Mrs. Prince, if the officer tries to ask you what it was I called to see you about, tell him nothing. You're just an ordinary member of the public and you don't have to answer any questions you don't want to. Remember what's likely to happen if they get the slightest suspicion of what's been going on."

"I'm not likely to forget."

I thought she could do it. She hadn't impressed me as the kind of woman who'd fly into a panic.

"What was the thing you remembered, by the way?"

"Oh, well it wasn't much, but you said anything. He—that man—once said something about having a girl friend who was a dancer."

A dancer. Well, that helped. Within twenty miles of Monkton, there probably weren't more than two or three hundred of those. Unless you counted in Hollywood.

"He didn't mention any name?"

"No. It isn't much help, is it?"

"Any little thing may help. And thank you for letting me know. Now you call your lawyer as soon as we hang up."

She promised to do it, and I cut the connection. There were now only seven minutes left before I was due at the Monteray Building, and Flower had said it was urgent.

I checked the clip on the ·38 before leaving the apartment.

It was nine thirty-five when I reached the Monteray, and this time I didn't call on the manager. Nobody was around as I entered the elevator and pushed the button marked "8". As I walked along to Apartment 824 I had the feeling I was going to learn something at last. The ·38 felt hard and reassuring against my side as I pressed the buzzer. The door opened almost immediately and there was Flower. Her face was white and drawn and she could barely force the words from her lips.

"Come in, come in."

I stepped inside. She backed away as though afraid I might strike her.

"What's this all——?" I started to say.

I didn't get any further. Somebody drove a steam-shovel against the side of my head. Great red explosions burst across my eyes as the floor boards leaped up to punch me in the face. My mind was slipping away. I thought a woman screamed, or maybe it was me, then somebody pulled down a thick black curtain and I crawled behind it.

CHAPTER SIX

I was climbing a mountain, but I didn't have the right boots and my feet kept slipping. My fingers scrabbled at the rock, and each time they achieved some kind of hold those feet betrayed me again. Gradually, I forced open an eye. The rock was a dirty gray color, only it wasn't rock. It was some kind of material. I closed the eye again and sighed. A man in my condition had no business climbing mountains in the dark. My fingers moved again. It was material. That seemed to justify another look with the eye, and this time I identified a chair two inches from my nose. The chair was the mountain. My mind was clearing now and I recalled where I was and how I got there. I was kneeling beside this chair, trying to pull myself upright. Flower. Flower had hit me on the head.

No, she hadn't.

I'd been looking right at her when it happened. Somebody else had done it, and that was why she was so afraid when I went in. This brilliant piece of reasoning made me feel quite smug, and I figured a smart character like me ought to be able to stand on his own feet. After two more trys I made it, just. There was no Flower here now. The guy with the steam-shovel was gone too, and that was a pity. I'd have liked to discuss the matter with him.

I lumbered around the apartment, but it hadn't any more to tell me than on my last visit. The window was wide open, and I went across to breathe some fresh air.

The night was that special purple when the stars look like decorations on some royal robe. It was a night for many things, none of which was getting slugged on the head. Down in the street below, somebody shouted. I looked down idly. There was a small crowd of people down there, looking up at me and pointing. Then I saw flashlights playing on something on the sidewalk. My head cleared like lightning as I realized what it was. It was the crumpled, twisted body of a woman, and although I couldn't see her face, I knew it had to be Flower. That was why all those people were pointing. Someone had probably seen her fall, and that meant I was the guy who pushed her. It was time to be going.

With a handkerchief I rubbed quickly at the door knob after I got outside, then the buzzer. There was nobody around, and according to my watch I'd been out of touch for about two minutes. That would hardly have given anyone time to identify the room and get up to it. The elevator light was on the move and was now at "4". It was a time for stairways, eight floors or no.

I went down fast pulling up at each storey level in case anyone was around. By the time I hit bottom I was reminding myself to cut down on the cigarets. There was nobody in the dim-lit entrance and I made good time out to where I'd parked the heap. I got inside and sat watching for a moment. The window through which I'd seen Flower was at the rear of the building, so all the excitement would be back there. My head gave me a twinge, reminding me that I'd been luckier than the girl. Wondered too, why I hadn't followed her through the window. I'd have been in no position to put up much of an argument about it. Still, here I was, and if I wanted to stay out of jail I'd better be moving. What I wanted was to go home and do something about my head, like maybe pour half a bottle of scotch inside it, but there was no

time for such indulgences. Instead I drove out to the
Beach End again.

Waves lapped softly against the silent sands as I passed
along the now deserted beach road. Even the waves had
to show a little respect down there. Other coarser sections
of the coast might get breakers and such, but here everything was orderly, straight out of your travel magazine.
The driveway to the Somerset house was brilliantly lit,
but the house itself was in darkness. But that didn't have
to mean it was empty. There could be some action around
back. I walked quietly around to where Flower had made
such a spectacular entrance that afternoon. The wide
glass doors stood open and although there was no light,
music flowed softly out into the night.

I peered into the gloom but couldn't seen anything.
On an impulse I stepped inside and the darkness was
total.

"You're late."

It was Somerset's voice and it seemed to come from
where I judged that long couch of his to be.

"Sorry," I replied. "I didn't realize I was expected."

"What the devil——"

A light snapped on and there he was again, still flat
on his back. Only this time he wore a glaring purple shirt
and bermuda shorts. And that wasn't all. In his hand was
a very large black ·44 revolver, pointed unwinkingly at
me.

"What is the meaning of this intrusion?" he demanded.

The words were more threatening than the voice. Instead he sounded somehow worried.

"Got some news for you," I told him. "Would you
mind putting that thing down?"

"Not until I know what you're doing here. You come
sneaking into my house in the middle of the night——"

"It's only just after ten o'clock," I corrected. "Will you put it down? Those things go off, you know."

He gave a short barking laugh.

"That is precisely what it is intended for," he assured me. "We get a lot of you burglars around this area."

"Oh don't be ridiculous."

I sat down, acting a lot calmer than I felt. He said uncertainly,

"You said you had something to tell me."

"You and Flower. Where is she, by the way?"

"How do I know, I'm not her keeper."

I looked at him and grinned.

"You could have fooled me."

He waggled the gun, then snorted and laid it on the floor beside him.

"Not that I can't reach it if I have to," he warned.

"You won't need it. Who are we expecting, anyway?"

"That's none of your business. Say what you have to say and please go away."

"O.K. Get Flower in here."

His face grew dark with bottled impatience.

"She isn't here. I don't own the girl, she comes and goes as she pleases. Tonight she pleases to be elsewhere. Do you understand?"

"And you don't know where?"

"I haven't the remotest idea. And if I had, I doubt whether I'd tell you."

We stared at each other with quiet hostility.

"Before I give you this fascinating news of mine, tell me one thing. Flower, is she some kind of dancer?"

"I don't see why I should tell you anything at all. But, if you must know, yes."

"Ah. And where were you an hour ago, Mr. Somerset? I telephoned here and got no answer."

"Then you must have dialled the wrong number.

There's only been one telephone call here the whole evening, and I answered that."

"Haven't been out, huh? Can you prove it?"

He frowned.

"Prove it?" he repeated. "No, I shouldn't think so. And I don't have to prove things to you. You can believe them or not believe them. It's a matter of supreme indifference to me."

"Yup, that's right. You don't have to prove a thing to me. Cops might take a different view though. They can be awful nasty."

He sighed and rubbed absently at the fleshy chest.

"And why should the police be interested?"

"Because of Flower. Somebody just killed her downtown."

He sat upright and the heavy eyes bored into me.

"You're lying," he said thickly.

"If you say so."

He sat quite still, then very slowly the bearded head wagged from side to side.

"It can't be true. Who told you this?"

"Nobody. I saw it."

"And there's no mistake."

It wasn't a question. The words were flat and monotonous.

"I think I'm going to need a drink."

For such a huge man he was very light on his feet as he moved across the room to the bar. He poured himself a great deal of vodka and drank it straight. Then he turned back to me, glass in hand.

"Tell me exactly what happened."

"It was outside Brookman's apartment. Did you know where he lived?"

He shook his head.

"Place called the Monteray Building. It isn't the Beach

End, but it's a little better than Conquest Street. Brookman lived on the eighth floor. Flower knew where he
lived all right. Because somebody opened a window on
that eighth floor and pushed her through."

He shuddered and emptied the glass. Immediately he
turned away and got the bottle to work again.

"And you actually saw it?"

"Not quite. I was just one of a crowd down at ground
level. But I couldn't have missed it by more than a
minute."

He came back and sat down heavily.

"Poor little Flower. And there was no harm in her at
all. Not real harm, nothing to call for this dreadful
thing."

He seemed more upset than I would have expected. But
then I can never be sure what to expect from anybody
any more.

"Did she live here?"

"No. I've no idea where she lived. She would come
when she wanted, and leave when she was ready. I don't
ask people where they live."

"Then you don't really know much about her?"

I must have sounded sceptical, because Somerset grinned
at me wryly.

"You don't understand, do you Preston? You, and
people like you don't understand. Where you come from,
everyone has to have a full name, address, occupation,
social security. They have to have a certain credit standing, high or low, but they must have it. Not everyone
in the world wants to be classified like that. Half the
people who come to this house, they exist only within
these four walls. Where they come from, who they are,
I don't know half the time. Flower was one of those."

"You're going to be a mine of information for the
police."

"I shall tell them what I can. If indeed they come to me."

I looked at him quickly.

"Why wouldn't they? You can bet they'll talk to everyone who ever laid eyes on her."

He nodded.

"Without doubt. But unless she happens to have my name written down in her purse, there's no reason why they should even think of me. Our connection was ten uous, to put it mildly. She didn't live here, didn't work for me. We haven't any real connection at all."

So he didn't need to concern himself. He could just go on lounging around listening to his music and chewing on his lotus, having tenuous connections with people who got shot in the head on clifftops, or pushed out of eighth storey windows.

"They'll be here," I promised, "And a lot rougher than last time."

"I see." He looked at me sideways. "Look, I appreciate the trouble you've taken coming out here to tell me about poor Flower. It's late at night, and I have a visitor coming. How would you like a thousand dollars?"

"I came out here," I told him siowly, "In the hope I'd catch you burning the papers, or whatever. To give it to you straight, Somerset, I'd a half-assed notion it could have been you killed her."

"And now?"

"I don't know what to think."

"A thousand dollars is a wonderful aid to clear thinking."

"No thanks, I already have a client."

"You could be important," he mused. "Yes very important, if this investigation gets out of hand. Let me help you think. What time did this thing happen?"

"Around nine forty—nine forty-five."

"And you came straight from there out to this house? Well, you needn't bother to answer. The distance involved and the time you arrived tells me that. You had to come directly here."

"So what does that prove?"

"I was already here," he pointed out.

"True. But you could have been here just five minutes ahead of me. Five seconds for that matter."

"Exactly. Now think, how did I get here?"

"We have things called automobiles these days. You could probably afford one if you saved your pennies."

"Good, good. I have three to be precise. You will find them out in the garage. And an experienced detective ought to be able to judge whether they've been out recently. Come."

I followed him out into the garden and round to the big white garage. He snapped switches and waved an arm.

"Help yourself," he invited.

I prowled around, laying hands on cold engines and exhaust pipes.

"None of these have been riding tonight," I admitted.

"Thank you. I could have come home on the trolley car of course, but we don't have a line out here."

Whether I liked it or not, I could not deny the very strong evidence that he was telling the truth. And the killer would hardly call a cab at the scene of the crime and have himself driven straight home.

"So why the thousand dollars?"

He leaned against the wall of the garage watching my inspection.

"Look at it from my point of view. Today, the police came. I was only one of a dozen people, possibly more. A routine enquiry into Brookman's death. By tonight they'll have realized I know nothing and they've probably written me off the books. But they will find it extremely odd if they have to come again tomorrow in connection with a second murder. Very odd indeed. Even in police work, I imagine coincidence has its reasonable limits. I'd like you to forget my involvement in this."

I patted the bonnet of a this year's shiny Cadillac.

"Save your money Mr. Somerset. Cops'll be here by morning, anyway."

He frowned quickly.

"You're determined to make trouble for me?"

"Not me. I won't say a word. And I'd appreciate it if you'd keep me out of this. You know, tit for tat?"

"Then how——"

Very patiently, I spelled it out for him.

"This is homicide. To you, a cop is a cop, and you see hundreds of them every day. But there are only a handful who deal with cases of homicide. It's routine that every man looks at the corpse where there's no identification, or even if there is. So the men who came to question you today will see Flower, either tonight or tomorrow morning. And they will remember where they last saw her. And they will be back to ask you what you know about it. Could I give you a small piece of advice?"

"I see. Yes, I see that," he muttered. "This is terrible. What did you say, advice? What kind of advice?"

"When they come, keep your thousand dollars in your pocket. They can get very stuffy about things like that."

But he wasn't listening. All the confidence had oozed out of him, and he was a badly worried man. I wondered why.

"Well I'd better get going. Wouldn't do for the law to find me here," I said, walking back outside. "They wouldn't like it if they thought I came straight to you instead of them. I might have saved them hours of work by identifying Flower."

"Yes, yes," he muttered absently.

76

I left him pacing disconsolately up and down as I drove away. Soon after I emerged on to the Beach Road another car came towards me. It was a powerful white Italian sports model, and the headlights were so bright I was momentarily dazzled. Slowing, I pulled over to the side of the road and watched my rear mirror. The newcomer swung into Somerset's driveway and disappeared from view. I thought about going back to find out who it was, decided against it.

The lump on my head wasn't contributing to the general gaiety, but I still had to make one more call before I hit the sack. Avoiding the center of town I headed out into the lightly wooded country on the far side. There was very little traffic around, and fifteen minutes I was on the quiet side road that led to Rose Suffolk's. Soon after that I was turning into the big forecourt, where colored spotlights played on the wood beam manor-house imitation that was one of the best night spots for miles around.

My first stop was in the men's room, where I washed up and tried to straighten my appearance. A wadded paper towel soaked in icy water made very good friends with my lump, and for a few blissful seconds the throbbing eased off. Then I was ready to make an appearance in public.

The bar was busy and I had to wait a while for service. All around me people seemed to be enjoying life. They were talking and laughing, taking an occasional sip. Here and there a young couple sat, perfectly content to be neither talking nor laughing, but simply looking at one another, which was enough in itself. Everybody in the whole wide world was with somebody else. Except me, naturally. My only company was a slowly returning throb in the head.

"It's bad for a man to drink alone."

I turned, and there was the proprietor in person, Rose Suffolk.

"Hallo Rose. Can I get you something?"

"Too early. I'll come and sit with you though, smoke one of your cigarets."

We threaded our way through, looking for a space to park. Several people spoke to her, and she had a word or a smile for each one. Finally I located a small table when the occupants were getting ready to leave. Another man tried to step in front of me but I used an elbow and he drew back, growling something about pushing people.

"That's good."

Rose settled back and relaxed. I made with the Old Favorites, and she inhaled luxuriously.

"That's good, too. You know Mark, I haven't been off my dogs since six-thirty. And there's still another four hours before we fold."

"Don't kid me, Rose. You love it."

I hadn't seen her in months but she still looked good as ever. In show business you can meet a hundred people before you encounter a smart one. Rose Suffolk was one of those. Originally a torch singer, she realized one day that she'd got as far as she was going. Not that she was unsuccessful, far from it. She played what they call in the trade the saloon circuit. And that does not mean a succession of crummy bars. It means the best night spots in every major city, a week here, two weeks there. She had a reasonable voice, and a tremendous style for putting a number across. Gradually she built up a repertoire of point numbers, for which she was best known. She was well thought of by the public and show people alike, but suddenly she realized life was set. At twenty-four she was at the top of her particular tree. There was no reason to suppose she couldn't go on exactly as she was for twenty more years, maybe longer. As she once put it to me, it dawned on her as she was doing the two a.m. spot at the Green Derby in Las Vegas. Looking at the people, and lapping up the applause she had a clear vision that one day she'd be going through the same routines for their children. And it did not appeal in the slightest. That was when she decided there was more to life than living in hotel rooms, even the best hotels, which they were. Earning top salary as she did, she began a saving campaign. She accepted all and any guest shots on television and radio, anything at all that helped to swell the bankroll. Then, when she was ready, she looked around for the right property. Rose was always a gal who knew exactly what she wanted and was content to wait until she found it.

"Aren't you going to talk to me?" she said suddenly. I realized my thoughts had been wandering.

"Sorry Rose, I was thinking. About you."

"Oh, well," she pouted, but considerably mollified. "What about me?"

"I was thinking about the old days, before you bought this place. Back then, there were only three girls for me. Ella, Peggy Lee and Rose Suffolk. Don't you miss it?"

"Oh sure, sometimes. It was a lot of fun, and naturally I miss a lot of it. But I'm my own boss here. If I want time off, I just take it. I'm not looking for any handouts, and short of a general depression I never will be, maybe not even with one. I have regular hours, not the same hours as everyone else perhaps, but regular. I haven't been in an airplane in months and when I eat, it isn't a quick sandwich and coffee in some airport lounge or on a train. Do I look bad on it?"

I couldn't have a better excuse to look at her, and she was well worth the looking. Her long shiny black hair was pulled flat against her head and tied in some kind of bun at the back. The finely chiselled face was tanned

79

a light brown, highlighting the warm redness of her mouth against the sparkling teeth. She wore a halter dress of red silk, gathered against the small firm breasts and hugging the slim waist before falling to the long slender legs.

"Wow!" I announced.

She chuckled.

"You see. I'm not so bad for an old retired lady. Which raises a point. If I'm so wow, how come you've played the duck for my place for so long?"

"I have a broken heart," I told her. "On account of the lady seems to be spoke for."

She nodded seriously.

"How well do you know Jake?"

"Not too well. Funny thing, I was sort of hoping I might run across him here tonight."

She wagged a finger.

"You see. Even now you didn't come to see me at all. You came on business."

"I didn't mention business," I cut in quickly.

"You didn't have to. With Jake, everything's business. The guy never relaxes."

"Better complain to him. He'll be here any minute."

She followed my gaze towards the entrance. Clyde F. Hamilton, the hoodlum with the family tree, was standing in the doorway. Rose turned and placed her lips close to my ear. I could have wished her motives had been different, but all she wanted was to whisper.

"Do you know Clyde?"

"Met him," I replied briefly.

"Funny thing about Clyde. He's good-looking, beautifully dressed, and his education would take him anywhere. But I can't get with him at all. I'll tell you Mark, the guy gives me the creeps."

I grinned to myself. There's a lot of hoo-hah talked

about women's intuition, but Rose's was a long street ahead of Florence Digby's.

"I don't have any opinion about him," I told her. "Only met the guy for a couple of minutes."

She looked at me shrewdly, but said nothing. Jake Martello had followed Hamilton inside and the heavy face creased into smiles as he caught sight of Rose. He waved and came over, Hamilton close behind.

"Rose sweetie, you look like a million."

"Hi Jake."

"Preston, you wouldn't be stealing a feller's girl, now would you?"

He was jocular, but there was a trace of anxiety behind the tone. Martello was widely known to have it very bad for Rose.

"Not me Jake. Just warming a seat till you got here."

"And I'm not your girl," snapped Rose.

I watched the glances between them, but could not decide whether they were kidding or not.

"Good evening Rose, Preston."

Nobody had spoken to Hamilton, so he thought he ought to get the ball moving himself.

"Hallo Clyde," said Rose coldly.

I nodded at him.

"Well now this is real nice," beamed Jake. "Only thing, we don't have enough chairs."

"Oh boy," said Rose disgustedly. "You should carry your own barn door to drop on people."

"Now, now honey you know I didn't——"

"It's all right." I got up. "I have to be going anyway. Tell you what, Jake, how would it be if we stepped out for a smoke. Your friend here can keep Rose company till you get back."

"Fine, fine. Suits me, Look after the lady, Clyde."

Hamilton sat down. Rose smiled up at me.

"I've never been stood up for a smoke before. You coming back?"

"No lady, I don't think so. I just don't have that wanted feeling."

"Preston here has class," voted Martello. "He knows when it's time to blow."

I winked at Rose and followed Jake out through the door. We stood out on the lighted porch, and he took a deep breath.

"Smell that air," he suggested. "What a night. A real beautiful night."

There was a flash among the parked cars. Jake grabbed at his heart and grunted. I put my arm around him and pulled him with me to the ground. A motor roared in the blackness and I strained my eyes towards the sound, but the gunman wasn't using any lights. "Clyde," muttered Jake. "Get Clyde."

CHAPTER SEVEN

I hurried back inside, Hamilton and Rose were sitting where I'd left them, not speaking. I bent over and kept my voice low.

"Jake's been shot. He wants you Hamilton. On the porch."

He got up fast, and gave me one swift vicious stare before going out. Rose had put her hand to her mouth and looked frightened.

"What happened?"

"We just got outside the door, a gun went off, Jake was hit."

"Is he—is it bad?"

"Can't tell. Is there a doctor here?"

She nodded and got up.

"I saw Dr. Andrews in the restaurant a little while ago."

"Get him, honey. And the law, get them too."

"All right."

I went back. One or two people stared at me curiously, wondering what all the comings and goings were about. Outside, Hamilton was kneeling beside his boss.

"He passed out. Looks like his heart, but I daren't touch him to find out."

"If he's still alive, it isn't his heart. That's one place that's guaranteed fatal. There's a doctor coming out."

I pulled out my Old Favorites and sucked down great belts of smoke. Hamilton stood up beside me.

"Is this your doing Preston?"

He said it quite conversationally, although we both knew an affirmative answer would be the same as a death warrant.

"No. We just got outside the door, and bang. It came from over among those cars."

"Then let's go take a look."

I pulled at his arm.

"No point. The guy drove off in a hurry as soon as Jake went down."

"Uh huh. How many shots?"

"Just the one."

"Pretty good. Doesn't sound like an amateur, does it?"

"It was a fair shot," I agreed. "But don't forget where we're standing. From out there we must have looked like a target in a fairground."

He pursed his lips and nodded.

"Fair comment. You could have set this up, even though you didn't do it yourself."

"Why would I want to?"

He grinned evilly.

"My dear Preston, I never concern myself with people's motives. I'm not some kind of welfare worker. I'm just interested in their actions. Like did you put Jake on the spot, or did you not."

"Not. Listen Hamilton, I don't have any more regard for you than you do me. But in a loose kind of way, we're about on the same side in this. The time might come we need each other. So cut out the amateur hawkshaw bit, and let's think about our visitors."

"Visitors?"

"Sure, police are on their way."

"Mr. Martello won't like that," he frowned. "But I can see it had to be done."

The door behind us opened, and Rose hurried out with a silver-haired, distinguished looking man.

"I'm a doctor," he announced briskly. "What's going on here?"

"This man's been shot," I told him.

He looked at me keenly and went down on his knees beside Jake.

"H'm."

Rose came and stood next to me, gripping my hand tightly.

"Have you called the police?" I whispered.

"Yes. Tell me Mark, is he very bad?"

Before I could answer the doctor straightened up.

"This man is in very bad shape. Is there an ambulance coming?"

"No," she hesitated. "I wasn't sure——"

"Get one Miss Suffolk, and quickly. I can't guarantee this man's life. And the police of course must be summoned."

Rose was already on her way to the phone. The doctor looked at Hamilton, then me.

"Are you friends of this man?"

"Yes."

"Does he have a family?"

I looked at Hamilton. He'd know best what Jake would want done.

"Just a brother, doctor."

"If you take my advice, you'll have that brother get over to the emergency ward in Monkton General."

"Right."

Hamilton went off to get in touch with Charlie Martello. Doctor Andrews said

"Would you mind if I had a cigaret? I left mine on the table."

"Certainly."

I held the flame for him and he nodded appreciatively. "This is a bad business. Did you see it happen?"

"I was with him."

I didn't want to get too chummy with the doctor. I really wanted to be left alone to get my thinking straight. If I wasn't very careful with my story, the whole Brookman thing would come out, and then I'd be in real trouble.

"Doctor, I'm feeling shaky. That bullet could just as easily have hit me. Would you mind if I went inside and got myself a drink? I could certainly use one."

"Make it brandy. Best thing in circumstances of this kind."

"I will."

I went in and headed for the room Rose used as an office. She was standing by the window, a tumbler in her hand. Hamilton was on the telephone.

"What's this all about, Mark? Who'd want to kill Jake?"

"I have no idea honey," I replied truthfully. "Let's hope whoever it was did a bad job."

She nodded and sipped at her drink.

"If I'm likely to spend half the night under interrogation, I could use a drink."

"Help yourself."

She waved towards the liquor cabinet. I splashed out a solid helping of scotch and gulped some down. Hamilton had finished his call now.

"Charlie is going to the hospital as the doctor suggested. He also wants to have speech with you, Preston."

"I imagine he will. Look Hamilton, it'll be all cops here in five minutes time. If you're wearing anything, I suggest you let Rose look after it for you. Unless you have a license, that is."

He nodded.

"Good thinking. Could I put you to the trouble, Miss Suffolk?"

She hadn't been listening.

"Huh, trouble? What trouble?"

He slid a hand inside his coat and produced a small black automatic. The movement was so smooth and fast it was a pleasure to watch him. It was also a fact I made a note to remember. Rose Suffolk gasped as he put the gun on the table.

"What's that for?"

"Just a silly habit I've dropped into," he replied easily. "Never been fired since the day I bought it. But it's a fact I haven't a license for it, and the police would have every right to bring some kind of charge against me, just for carrying it. So if you wouldn't mind?"

She didn't believe him, and turned to me.

"I don't understand this, Mark. Should I do what he says?"

"Yes, Rose, I think you ought. If Jake's going to be laid up for a spell, he's going to need Hamilton looking after things for him."

That made sense. She went across and opened an old-fashioned wall safe behind a picture.

"Put it in there," she said flatly.

Hamilton walked across, and with evident reluctance slipped the gun inside. Rose closed the door and twirled the knobs. Then she slid the picture back in position. In the distance now we heard the mournful wail of a siren.

"We'd better get outside with Jake," I suggested.

We all trooped out to where the doctor stood, quietly smoking.

"Everything's arranged now," I told him.

He nodded, without speaking. The siren was loud now, and a minute or so later a sleek blue ambulance slid to a halt a few feet away. A white-coated intern dashed out, with a bag in his hand. Seeing Andrews, he pulled up.

"Oh good evening sir. Have you examined the patient?"

"Yes doctor. Gunshot wound immediately above the heart. Some loss of blood, and I suspect internal bleeding. It's an emergency operation I'm afraid."

"I ought to get some details. . . ." he hesitated.

"Look, the police are coming here at any minute," I interrupted. "The important thing is to get this man into hospital. His name is Martello, J. J. Martello. Mr. Hamilton here will be down to see you later to give you all the information you need.'

"Well, I guess it's all right," said the intern doubtfully.

"I'm Rose Suffolk, doctor," she cut in. "I can assure you everything will be in order."

He smiled at her, the way men always did.

"Oh well, if you say so Miss Suffolk."

The stretcher men were there by this time and they loaded Jake into the back of the waggon.

"Dr. Andrews, did you wish to come sir?"

"No thank you doctor, I'm sure the patient is in good hands."

"Yes sir. Thank you sir."

Dr. Andrews was evidently somebody who drew a lot of water in medical circles. Having an emergency involving both him and the delectable Rose Suffolk was something the young doctor would remember a long time.

The noise of the ambulance had drawn a number of people outside, and they were chattering excitedly and staring at the four of us.

"Perhaps if there's somewhere a little more private Miss Suffolk?" suggested Andrews.

"Certainly doctor. We'll go into my office."

We all trooped in, ignoring the questions fired at us. Inside the office nobody was in the mood for chatter.

We sat, well spaced out around the room, and that's where we were when the police arrived. It had to be Randall of course, and with him one Schultz, now Detective First Grade. They both saw me at the same time, and looked at each other with resignation.

"Well, well, Mr. Preston isn't it? You sure get around."

Randall studied me unlovingly, I shrugged and ignored him. He switched his attention to the others. He got all the names, Schultz scribbling away on his little pad. After that he asked Dr. Andrews half a dozen questions, thanked him for his cooperation, and let him go. The stuff with the doctor was no more than a formality, now he could get down to the real work. Half an hour later he said tiredly

"All right, now this is the way it stacks up. Please interrupt me if I have anything wrong."

He ran over it from the beginning, and being Randall there wasn't even a comma out of place. At the end we all agreed he had it right and he nodded.

"Very well. We shall have to get corroborating testimony from people outside, but as I see it of this moment you Miss Suffolk and you too Mr. Hamilton are more or less bystanders. You on the other hand Mr. Preston," and he underlined the "Mr." with heavy sarcasm, "You are in a very different situation."

I didn't need him to tell me that. If Jake Martello died, there would be no one around to support my statement that there ever was any gunman out in the night.

"Yes, a very different situation. I know it isn't relevant, but you possess an automatic pistol, a ·38 caliber Police Special, if memory serves me correctly. Do you have it with you?"

"Yes."

"Perhaps you wouldn't mind if I had a look at it?"

I handed it over and he inspected it.

"This certainly hasn't been used tonight," he grumbled.

"It hasn't been used in more than a week," I informed him. "Could I have it back please?"

Reluctantly, he passed it over.

"Rourke will be wanting to see you," warned Randall. "And you'd better be praying that Martello pulls out of this. The Captain don't like solitary witnesses to mysterious shootings on dark nights. They make him nervous. Especially when it's their idea for the victims to go out in the dark in the first place."

I hadn't anything to say on that. If I annoyed Randall, he had plenty of justification for taking me in, and that was the last thing I wanted. Finally, he gave it up. Then he and Schultz went outside to get some independent witness material, and we all looked at each other.

"Much as I dislike policemen, which is plently, I have to admit the big fellow works well," announced Hamilton.

"Right," I assented. "And don't ever underestimate him. Lots of people get the notion Randall's asleep on his feet, because he looks so tired all the time. And lots of people are wrong."

"I could tell you and he were old-er-friends?" he nodded. "That was interesting wasn't it, the way he hoped, Mr. Martello would recover for *your* sake? Yes, a smart one, that."

"I thought we more or less agreed to cut it out, a while back," I grumbled. "Are you going down to the hospital to help fill out all those forms?"

He got up, stretching himself tiredly.

"I suppose I'd better. If I could trouble you to open the safe, Miss Suffolk?"

He looked at her in polite enquiry. I had the feeling Rose didn't like her boy friend's assistant too well, but she certainly couldn't fault him on the way he addressed her. It was like a graduation exercise from a school of deportment. Crossing to the safe she waited pointedly for him to look away while she dialled the combination. Then she motioned for him to take out the gun himself.

"Thank you."

He slid the weapon back inside his jacket with satisfaction. From what I'd seen of Hamilton and people like him, I doubted whether he was ever separated from his gun for any length of time. I had an idiotic vision of him with a padded pyjama jacket and smiled inwardly.

"Did Charlie say when he wanted to see me?" I queried.

"Never fear. He'll be in touch after he's through at the hospital."

Hamilton nodded to us and went out. In the doorway he passed the anxious figure of Rose's floor manager. He came in looking distinctly flustered.

"Miss Suffolk, I'm afraid the crowd are rather restless," he said apologetically. "Everybody keeps demanding to know what happened, and they want to hear it from you personally."

Rose smiled and sighed.

"What you mean is, get out there and sing 'em quiet?"

He shrugged.

"I'm sorry. I know how you must be feeling. But there's some of our best customers out front, and they don't come all this way just to talk to me."

She stood up, and so did I.

"You see the way it is Mark, the show must go on, like the man said. You want to come and watch?"

"Ordinarily, there's nothing I'd like better. But there are several things I ought to be doing. I think Jake would prefer me to be doing them."

"I understand. You'll be careful won't you? And if there's anything I can do, anything at all."

"You bet. And I'll let you know if I hear anything that would interest you."

Gravely, she patted me on the cheek.

"Take care, boy." Then she turned to the manager. "All right my friend. Let's get this show on the road."

As I went out I heard the sudden roar of applause that greeted her appearance. Alone in the lighted porchway, I felt the quick clutch of fear at my throat, in case the gun artist was back at the same old stand. But nobody shot me as I walked nervously to the car and slipped inside.

CHAPTER EIGHT

Despite what I'd said to Rose Suffolk I hadn't any am-
bition to get into further trouble that night. One murder
and one shooting, both with me present, were enough to
constitute a fair evening's work where I come from. So
I was feeling bushed when I pulled up at Parkside Towers.
I looked at the gleaming structure without love. If the
place didn't slap such a high rental on me, I could be
taking fewer risks in the curious calling I like to describe
as my trade. Still, I reflected, that was just the bile in
my system showing through. Every now and then I tell
myself all this pushing around I get is solely for the benefit
of the owners of the Towers. But it isn't true. I stay there
because I like the place, because it shows people how far
I've come since the early days of a one-room flop in
Crane Street. And besides, if a man has to collect a bruise
now and then, he may as well nurture it in comfortable
surroundings.

"Preston."

My mental soliloquy was disturbed by a jarring rusty
voice, I swivelled towards a short thick man in a panama
hat. It looked ridiculous on him, but that was all about
him that was at all ridiculous. He looked like a guy with
no sense of humor, and he hadn't got his hand in a right
pocket because of the cold night air. He was a stranger.

"Who are you?" I demanded.

"It doesn't matter. Mr. Martello wants to see you."

I looked at his face to see if he was kidding, knowing

93

it to be a waste of time. This one never kidded anybody in his whole life.

"I don't get it. Call back tomorrow," I suggested.

"Not tomorrow. Now."

He moved his hand significantly inside the pocket.

"Look," I said, "Whatever it is you want, I don't buy it. And if you think I'm going anywhere with you, you're crazy. And you can stop pushing that thing at me. That suit cost you two hundred bucks at least. You're not going to shoot holes through the pocket. And by the time you take the gun out, I'll have smeared you all over the sidewalk. So it's a stand-off. Run away."

The slate eyes glinted, and he seemed almost amused.

"Smart, ain't you? But Mr. Martello knows how to look after the smart ones. You better come."

Wearily, I said:

"Look, buddy boy, don't give me that Martello come-on. Jake is over in the General Hospital. He's been shot and he isn't calling for anybody. And if he wanted me, he'd know there's no need for any muscle. So why don't you go away before I start slapping you around?"

He nodded.

"So that's it. A misunderstanding. We start again. I'm from the other Mr. Martello, Mr. Charlie Martello. Does it make a difference?"

"Well of course it does. You just stop waving the howitzer, and tell me where I find him."

The change of tone made him uncertain. Reluctantly he took a thick hand from his pocket. The hand was empty.

"Gee, I don't know," he muttered. "Boss said you might give me an argument.'

"Bosses make mistakes," I assured him. "Which way?"

"I'm in the blue Ford," he pointed. "You want to follow me?"

"Why not?"

He drove slowly, uncertain at intersections, like someone who was a stranger to the city. After a few minutes he pulled in outside one of the new hotels down near the beach. I got out and walked up to him.

"After you," I waved.

He shook his head, mumbling something under his breath. I had a feeling he was disappointed at the way I was making everything so easy for him. I guess if you're a muscle-man and nobody will let you use your muscles, it could induce a Freudian experience.

We went up to the third floor and he took off the panama, rapping on a door. It was opened from inside and we went in. Charlie Martello was standing by the window, and as the door closed behind me I turned to see another stranger who'd forgotten how to smile. Clyde Hamilton sat easily in an armchair looking at me steadily.

"So you came."

Charlie spoke the words half over his shoulder. The voice was almost entirely devoid of expression.

"Sure. You asked me," I replied.

"That's right, I asked you," he confirmed. "Why do you suppose I did that? I mean I ain't throwing no tea-party or nothing?"

"I imagine you want to talk about Jake."

Now he turned, quite slowly and impressively. I could imagine there were people in San Francisco who had reason not to feel too good when Charlie Martello turned in their direction like that.

"Right again. It's good the way you get so many things right," he nodded. "I want to talk about Jake. I want to talk about how come you pulled Jake out of a safe place into a nice firing range and somebody put a hole in him. I want to talk about why he's down at the hospital and you're still walking around. As of this minute," he added, as an afterthought.

I could have managed without the afterthought.

"There's nothing I can tell you," I assured him. "We stepped out there, this gun went off, a car drove away."

"Just like that."

He spaced the words out evenly and emphatically.

"That's how it happened."

He nodded and eyed me carefully from head to toe. None of the others moved.

"Now hear this," he continued, stabbing a thick forefinger at me. "That's my brother they got down there. I want to hear more from you, a whole lot more. And if you don't talk pretty, we'll see how a little shoe leather around the mouth works out."

I didn't like the feel of things at all. There were four of them, and big hero as I sometimes think I am, I would have about an even rating with a snowball on a hot fire.

"I don't know what else I can tell you."

I tried to sound unconcerned.

"You can start with the little trick you used to get him out there."

"That wasn't any trick," I snorted. "The guy is paying me. He's entitled to know what I'm doing for his money. You were there this morning. You heard me tell him I might look him up at Rose's."

"Uh."

He moved his teeth around inside a closed mouth, as though chewing on something unpleasant.

"So what were you going to tell him?"

"I'm working for Jake," I said doggedly. "Man hires somebody private like me, he wants it kept that way."

A slow, unpleasant grin came over the heavy lips.

"Brother, you're just asking for a work out ain't you? Jake's not taking no interest now, so tell me."

My late escort and the other goon took a step nearer to me.

"Things being the way they are, I guess I'll have to tell you," I shrugged.

"Good. Now we're getting someplace," he breathed.

"But only you. I'm not shouting Jake's business out in front of these clowns. Get rid of them if you want to hear it."

Again there was silence while everybody present looked at Charlie Martello. He bit at a fleshy thumb, spat out a piece of finger nail to the carpet.

"O.K. You guys wait in the next room."

His two henchmen moved obediently away. I jerked a thumb at Hamilton.

"He goes, too."

Hamilton didn't flicker an eyelid, merely watched his boss's brother.

"Why him?" demanded Charlie.

"Because he doesn't like me, and it's mutual. Because I'm going to tell you something that could get me into a lot of trouble. And he might take it into his head to use it for just that."

"And you think I won't?"

"I have to trust somebody. And you're Jake's brother."

He twitched his head, and Hamilton got up. Before leaving the room he treated me to a malevolent stare.

"Mind, this don't make no difference," warned Charlie. "I don't like what I hear, you could still get pushed around."

The man was dangerous. Somebody put a hole in his brother, and he wanted something done about it, something physical and quick. I was the nearest candidate for that kind of exercise, and I wasn't looking for election.

"I'm still waiting."

I began to tell him. Names were the only parts I left
out. For the mood Martello was in, he was quite capable
of undertaking a grand tour with his goons, beating up
everybody I'd spoken to that day.

"And that's all?"

"I thought it was a pretty tight schedule for one day's
work."

"H'm. You never told me no names."

"I always make my reports that way," I lied.

"So how do you figure it? Which of these people
shot Jake?"

I held up a hand.

"Whoa," I remonstrated. "Too fast, much too fast.
Maybe none of them. Remember, I didn't see everybody
yet. And there could be others, lots of others, I may not
even have heard of. It's too early for calling names.

"That's on the level, about the dame got herself knocked
off?"

"It is."

Without moving he leaned across and switched on a
radio. Shrill music blared into the room. I didn't like that
too well. Where I come from, some people switch up
radios while they lean on other people. The music drowns
out other noises. Like scream noises. The door opened
fast and Hamilton came in, followed by the others. Martello turned irritably.

"Nobody needs ya. Get outa here."

They went sheepishly away, while Charlie fiddled with
the radio dials. Finally he got away from music and on
to a man speaking.

"——followed by a newscast in just four minutes
time."

Martello grunted and turned to me.

"We got four minutes. Take the weight off."

I sat down in the chair Hamilton had vacated. The man

on the radio droned away with a message of peace and love for the brotherhood of man. If the message was getting through to brother Charlie, there was nothing on his face to betray the fact.

Four minutes doesn't sound very long, but the seconds seemed reluctant to slip away unnoticed. Each one seemed to quiver petulantly on my watch before sliding across to make way for the next. I tapped out an Old Favorite and pushed it in my face. The smoke was hot and unfriendly in my throat, and I was about to stub the cigaret when I changed my mind. If I were to do that just after it was lit, Martello might think I was nervous or something. How wrong can a man be?

He hadn't moved, just stood by the window, waiting for four minutes of his life to ebb away.

" . . . to that great day when all men will walk forward together, shoulder to shoulder, and with heads held high. . . ."

I was beginning to hate the guy on the radio. Then quite suddenly the droning ceased. Some people sang a little jingle about how crispy certain candy bars were.

"And now it's newstime on your station of the stars. In Vietnam this afternoon. . . ."

Charlie turned up the volume so the guy in the next apartment could learn what was going on in the world.

" . . . at the United Nations. . . ."

At least I needn't bother with a newspaper next morning. The items wore on, overseas, political, labor news. Then

"and for our last item, a special interview with the senior police officer investigating the mysterious death today of lovely Serena Fenton. Miss Fenton appears to have fallen from the eighth floor of the Monteray Apartment Building here in Monkton City. A special feature of the enquiry is that the apartment was that formerly occupied by Poetry Brookman, shot to death last night at Indian Point."

Charlie switched off. I was disappointed. I'd been hoping to hear who the senior police officer was. Probably some front man for the department. They'd never let any of Rourke's squad loose on the air.

"So it checks," murmured Charlie. "That far it checks."

"If those guys ever found out I was there, they'd have my license," I told him.

"That's tough. If I ever find out you're lying to me, I'll break you're neck," he said off-handedly. "So what happens now?"

"Looks like your play," I pointed out.

"Ah."

He slapped at his leg with irritation.

"I never figured you except as a right guy. Trouble is, I'm all mixed up. Back home now, things'd be different. I know everybody, everbody knows me. Back home I'd have that town upside down. You wouldn't be able to go to the can without I'd know. But here——" he spread his arms "——I'm like some visiting fireman. I ought to be out cracking a few heads, that's what."

It was the nearest I was going to get to an apology. But I knew the signs. Preston was off the hook.

"Everybody's working on it," I assured him. "And I have a lot of calls to make. Especially now."

"Now? You mean because of Jake?"

He eyed me beadily, sceptical that I should be particularly worried if somebody shot his brother.

"No, not really because of Jake. Because of me. I've been doing a lot of thinking. Who's stirring up all this trouble over the Brookman murder? Jake? No, it's me.

I'm the one asking all the questions, poking my nose all over this village. Why would anybody want to kill Jake? Remember, there were two of us outside that joint to-night. Jake's the one who got shot, but who's to know which one was aimed at?"

He let out breath in a long low hiss.

"Yeah. Yeah, I hadn't figured that angle. You could be right, Preston. And you're the one can prove that Fenton dame was murdered. Nobody else could swear she wasn't alone up there." I nodded.

"That's the way I've been stacking it up."

He pondered for a moment.

"Yeah, but hold it. If that's true, why didn't they take care of you when they killed the dame? Don't make sense, leaving it till later."

I'd been wondering about that myself, and thought I had an answer.

"Because I wasn't expected. It's not easy to kill a full-grown-man in a short time unless you have a gun or a knife. Whoever it was killed the girl went there expecting to have nothing else to do but push her out of a window. It's a different proposition trying to heave a guy my size up off the floor."

He thought about it, nodding slowly.

"Yeah, that figures. It was your lucky day the guy wasn't heeled, huh?"

"I guess so."

There was another silence, and I decided it was time for home. Unless Charlie had other ideas.

"Well, it's pretty late," I said. "If you don't want me any more——?"

"Eh?—oh, no, no. You blow, Preston. Keep in touch, huh?"

"Will do."

I didn't bother about farewells for Hamilton and the

others. In my business there's a time to get, and when that time comes I don't stand on any ceremony.

Back in the car I wrote down Martello's telephone number, which I'd taken a peek at while I was with him. It was my last task of the day. Whatever else was to be done would have to wait till morning. I was bushed.

CHAPTER NINE

Next morning I got up around nine and paddled around making coffee and coughing over my first cigaret. The paper was full of stuff about Flower's murder and the shooting of Jake Martello. Jake was described as a financier, and I guess that's as good a word as any. I got a two word mention as "a friend" who was with him at the time, and that was all the publicity I needed for today. There was a lot of filler about Jake, and the club, and Rose Suffolk, and just about everything else the reporter could dream up. They gave him a column and a half, and all it said was Jake got shot and nobody knew who did it. With Flower they had a better deal. They now knew there was a connection between her death and the Brookman murder and they gave it plenty of treatment. The only disappointment from the paper's standpoint was the lack of any real evidence that she didn't fall naturally. Still, there was a rehash of the Brookman story, and plenty of emphasis on the mysterious connection with both cases of "the well-known entrepreneur Hugo Somerset."

I chuckled as I read that "entrepreneur" again. A word that covered a multitude of activities, not to say sins. Just the same, it was clear Somerset would be getting his fair share of questions from Randall and the others. Not that I was sorry about that. All the time they spent asking other people questions was time they couldn't spend darkening my door.

On an impulse I telephoned the hospital, and was told Jake Martello was making slow progress. I asked if they'd dug out the slug, and a frosty female voice advised me to ask his relatives. That I was not proposing to do at that hour of the morning. I didn't want to be around Charlie and his playmates anymore than was absolutely necessary.

I was very sharp today in my new brown mohair suit and knitted tie. Anybody would take me for a lawyer, or one of those respectable people. An architect maybe, I thought as I admired myself in the mirror by the front door. Of course, architects don't carry ·38 Police Specials under their nice mohair jackets, I reflected glumly as I opened the door. Once again I found myself heading for Conquest Street. This is one of the more interesting streets in our fair city. It starts off close to the business section, with a legitimate theater right on the corner. That's where it starts, how it starts. After that each succeeding group of buildings slides further and further down the social scale, and every other kind of scale. Half a mile along there are the girlie shows, clip-joints, run-down gym, every kind of entertainment you could put a name to, especially that kind. At nights, Conquest is no place to leave a car, but at that hour of the morning I knew most of the quick-money boys would be getting their hard-earned rest. I turned into a side-street and got out, locking up carefully. On the sidewalk a heap of rags groaned and stirred. A bony arm poked out from the heap and waved feebly from side to side before disappearing back among the rags. That'll give you some idea of the atmosphere around that end of Conquest.

I found the building I wanted, and learned that Art Green—Impressario was on three. From the amount of stairs I climbed I was beginning to wonder whether that should have read thirty three. But I made it finally, and found myself standing before a peeled door with A—T

G - - - N barely discernible in dirty white capitals. It didn't say anything about impressario, and maybe the sign-writer ran out of paint about there.

Nobody took any notice of the first knock, so I gave the door a second application and this time there was movement and grumbling from inside.

"Go away."

That was no way for an impressario to impress prospective clients.

"Open it up," I called through the door.

Then I gave it a couple of kicks to show I wanted in.

"All right, all right, you don't have to knock the place down."

A bolt scraped and I got my first look at Mr. Green. I don't know a lot about show business, but from where I stood he didn't look like any Ziegfeld. He was a short skinny guy, with a near-yellow face and blue stubble to make it more colorful. His top teeth were almost as yellow as his face. I couldn't tell about the lower half because he hadn't put them in yet.

"What's the idea?" he snapped.

"Mr. Green?" I enquired politely.

"That's what it says," he replied, not so politely. "Whaddya mean, dragging a guy outa bed middla da night?"

I looked through the landing window at the strong sunlight. Maybe Mr. Green normally wore eyeglasses too.

"Want to talk to you. Do I come in, or would you sooner I shouted my business all over the street?"

If I knew anything about people who lived that end of Conquest, that kind of publicity was the last thing Mr. Green would want. His eyes took on a furtive look and he peeked quickly outside to make sure there was no one around.

"Like that, huh?" he said hopefully. "Sure, sure. Come

in if you want. Why should you care if I never get any sleep."

I stepped inside, and the close atmosphere made my nostrils react sharply.

"What do you do for air?"

He shrugged.

"Listen, me I like fresh air. I believe in it. But to have air, you gotta have open windows. And believe me, anybody around here leaves a window open at night, he's crazy. Why, some of those guys wouldn't leave the strings in your shoes."

To show what a fresh-air fiend he was, he yanked open a big window and I felt safe in taking a breath. We were in a room about fourteen by twelve, and this seemed to be the extent of the Green holdings. In one corner stood a folding bed, and at the far end a drab curtain was pulled to one side, showing the catering arrangements.

Green stood in his undershirt, picking at his few teeth, and eyeing me curiously.

"So, you're in," he pointed out.

"Right. This is your lucky day, Art. Today, you make a profit."

"Um."

He didn't sound too excited about it. There had to be more, and somewhere in that more would be the catch the Art Greens of this world have learned to expect.

"You don't seem very pleased," I reproved.

"Pleased? What's to be pleased?" he cackled. "You come bustin' in here in the middla the night, talking about profits. Way I hear it, a guy has to make an investment before he gets around to a profit. Investments I don't need today. What's your pitch?"

"It seems there's a girl, a girl I want to meet."

"Ah."

Now I was getting a reaction. Girls made sense, even

at that hour of the morning. Girls have been around a long time, and all the time they've been around, there's been an Art Green with some kind of corner on the market. Now the profit began to look more of a reality.

"What kind of girl would you have in mind?" he asked softly.

"Would it matter?"

I winked him one of my all-boys-together winks and he looked positively cheerful.

"Why no, as a matter of fact, it wouldn't matter at all," he assured me.

"Just state your preference, give me five minutes to make a phone call and you are in business."

I smiled.

"Great. Matter of fact, I do have a special girl in mind. Her picture was in the paper. Shiralee O'Connor is the name."

All happiness faded from his face. A new expression took it's place, and to me it looked like fear.

"I don't believe I know——" he began.

"Oh, but you do," I interrupted. "I saw a mock-up of the story in the Globe Office. The original photograph was pinned to it. And your name was on that picture, Art."

He took a step away from me, as though he'd been threatened.

"Photograph?" he muttered, "There must be some——"

"No mistake," I cut in. "You're my boy, Art. Tell me where to find her."

"Listen, that poor kid's had a tough time over that," he pleaded. "All the time cops and reporters with nothing but questions."

"I could see she was the shrinking violet type," I sneered. "Just get that address up."

Then he decided on a different approach, and grew aggressive.

"Say what's it to you anyhow? You can't go around interfering with private citizens. What gives you the right to come here pushing me around?"

"Nobody's pushing you around, Art," I corrected. "Though it could probably be arranged if you weren't feeling cooperative."

He backed further away till he felt the bed behind him. Then in one quick movement he dived under the pillow and came up with an old army colt.

"Yeah?" He was ten feet tall now. "Who's gonna push who around? You just get out of here before I mistake you for some kind of burglar."

The gun didn't look to me as though anyone had fired it in twenty years. I walked slowly to the only chair and sat down. He watched me with rising impatience.

"Listen, I told you——"

"Art, Art." I remonstrated sadly. "That's all foolish talk, and you know it. There are some people, not many, who can shoot a stranger down in cold blood. You're not one of those people, so why don't you stop clowning around, and let's talk?"

He lowered the gun, but didn't put it down.

"I got nothing to say," he said sullenly.

"Sure you have. You're going to tell me where I find her. And then you're going to pick up those."

I tossed two tens on the office table and he licked his lips. But he shook his head firmly.

"No can do. Go ask the cops. You got any business with the girl, maybe they'll tell you."

"But I don't want to go to the cops," I pointed out. "They might ask who sent me. And then I'd have to say it was you, and when they asked about you I'd have to tell them you were a guy who supplied girls for parties.

Why, I might even have to tell them you offered to promote one just for me alone. You wouldn't want me to do that?"

"That's a lotta hooey," he scoffed. "They wouldn't take just your word."

"Right. But they'd come around and ask questions. You got all the answers, Art? About the parties, and where the money goes, stuff like that? You keep a nice set of books for the Internal Revenue boys? They like books you know. And maybe there's a little blackmail going for you too, on the side. No, you're right. They may not take my word, but they'd certainly want a nice long talk with you."

He dropped the gun on the bed and passed a weary hand over the blue stubble.

"I knew I should never have answered that door," he groaned. "What did I ever do to you?"

"Nothing," I assured him. "Nothing at all. Now, why don't we keep it that way? Just come up with what I want, keep the money, you may never see me again."

"I should be so lucky," he grumbled. "All right, suppose I do tell you, what do you do then?"

"I go away. That's all you need to know."

"Maybe that's the best thing for me. Look, I'm taking an awful chance for twenty lousy bucks."

"What kind of a chance?"

He hesitated, as though he were afraid of something.

"You see this dame, this O'Connor, she has a guy kind of looking out for her. He told me to keep my mouth shut about where she lives.

"So? You already told the police and every newspaper in town."

He shook his head in denial.

"No. Cops, yes. I hadda tell them. When those guys ask, you tell if you got any brains. This feller, he understands that. The reporters just followed the fuzz. But you're different."

"And what's this terrible chance you're taking? You mean this guy will come visiting?"

"Could be. He has an awful mean temper."

Somewhere at the back of my mind a name sounded, but it was probably too much to hope for.

"Well all right Art, tell you what we do. You say I got rough with you, and you had to tell me. Would it sound more convincing if I laid one or two on you?"

He jumped.

"No, that won't be necessary. But thanks for the offer. Yeah that oughta keep him off me."

"Then how about the address?"

He went to the table and tore yesterday's date off the calendar. On the back he quickly scribbled with a stub of pencil. As he handed the paper over he scooped up the two bills and stuffed them in a pocket. I put the address away and got up.

"Nice to do business with you, Art."

"Likewise. Only do me a favor and forget to come back, willya?"

I smiled at him pleasantly and left him to get on with all his big deals.

CHAPTER TEN

The Palm Beach Apartments are not everything the name would lead you to suppose. There wasn't very much of Florida grandslam about the place, in fact there wasn't much of anything at all. Despite the high faluting title it was tucked away in a fairly respectable street in the residential section. It wasn't exactly Beverly Hills, and then again it wasn't Crane Street. Just an ordinary middle price kind of place, with the anonymous look that betokened traffic in, traffic out, nothing permanent. Shiralee O'Connor, according to my information, was to be found on the sixth floor, apartment 614. With relief, I found the elevator was in working order today, and rattled my way up to six. There was nothing about the door to say who was on the other side, and I wondered whether Art Green's bad-tempered friend was around.

The bell made musical sounds inside, and I straightened my tie, recalling the photograph in the Globe. The door opened and I looked at a young tired woman wrapped in a flannel robe. She waited.

"Miss O'Connor?"

"Another reporter," she said disgustedly. "I already said all there is to say."

"No, not this time. I'm making a few enquiries and you may be able to help. I'd be glad to pay for your time."

"Yeah?" she didn't believe it. "My time is worth twenty bucks an hour."

I produced a ten and wagged it.

"How's for about thirty minutes? Maybe less."

"I don't know," she said doubtfully. "You could be some kind of crum. Those pictures in the newspapers."

I flashed my sticker and she nodded.

"Cop huh? Well I guess it's all right."

I followed her inside and she closed the door.

"Just making some coffee," she invited.

"Thanks. Black."

I sat on a cane chair while she went through a door and banged cups carefully. The coffee smelled good.

"Brother, what a night," she wailed.

"Work late?"

"Late?" she shrugged. "What's late? So long since I went to bed in the dark I forgot what the word means. Say I must look an awful mess."

She put a hand to the uncombed hair and waited for me to contradict her. I grinned.

"Let's put it this way, you're not entirely ready for any handout stills right this minute."

She made a face, then chuckled ruefully.

"You're not so bad. You gotta sense of humor. This I like. Now, what is it you want to know? Got a cigaret?"

I fumbled for my Old Favorites and she leaned over to get a light. The robe fell partly open, but she didn't bother to grab at it. I didn't get the feeling it was a come-on. It was just that when a girl has danced a few hundred private parties that kind of thing isn't important any more.

"That's good."

She leaned back, inhaling deeply, and studying me at the same time.

"What was that name, Preston? Mark Preston?"

"It was."

"I heard it some place."

"Maybe. Look Shiralee—may I call you that?"

"My friends call me Pook."

"All right then, Pook. I'm looking around to find out who killed this man Brookman."

She snorted.

"You and everybody else in town. I can't tell you much."

"Perhaps not. But I can't overlook anything, anybody. How well did you know him?"

"I didn't know him at all," she denied. "O.K. if they say he was at Hugo's he was there. But the first I ever heard of him was when the law came banging on the door."

"I see. Was it a big party?"

"You know Hugo—or do you?"

"I've talked with him."

"He throws these wingdings, people wander in and out the whole time. I guess there was twenty people there, thirty. Maybe more. I'm not so hot at figures."

I thought I heard a movement from the second door, the one that didn't lead into the kitchen, which would make it the bedroom.

"But after you saw his picture, did you recognize him then?"

"No, that's what they kept asking. Now honestly, I've been dancing all over the state for nearly two years. One thing I learned a long time ago, never look at their faces. The look on most of 'em would scare a girl half to death. I can't help you mister."

I sipped at the scalding coffee. It was an excuse to listen for any more sounds from the bedroom. Nothing.

"I guess you're right. Thanks for trying. Keep the ten anyhow, the coffee was worth it."

She smiled, and I got a quick glimpse of the girl in the photograph. At the door I turned and said clearly.

"By the way, you know a man named McCann?"

No smile now, her face froze and she pointed to the door.

"I can't help you, I said. Beat it."

"No, no, honey, that ain't polite."

The bedroom door had opened and there stood Legs McCann.

"Well, well," I muttered. "This is a big surprise, Legs."

"I can imagine. I thought I knew the voice when you were giving honeybunch the con."

"That was no con. I need information."

He advanced into the room.

"You didn't get your full thirty minutes. Come on back in, and let's have a little loving talk."

"Why not?"

I went back and sat down again. Shiralee looked from one to the other fearfully.

"You guys know each other?"

"Sort of," he replied. "He ain't a real cop, he's private."

I hadn't seen him in a year or so, but there was no great change in him. He'd be, let's see, thirty two or three now, and good-looking in a florid way. McCann was always way out in front on two counts, his quick fists and a smooth way with the dames. Judging by appearances, he hadn't lost any of his old technique, and from the way he moved I'd have said he was still keeping in shape. Legs had been on the muscle for the bookies for years, and I could remember one time it took four policemen to calm him down when he was being pinched. I never knew him to carry a gun, but I noticed today he kept one hand in his pocket.

"You knew I was here," he accused.

"Wrong. I thought there was an outside chance you could tie in with this somewhere. I just tried the name out on Pook here as a long shot. Sometimes they pay off."

"H'm."

He didn't know whether to believe it or not. Either way it didn't matter. Here we all were, and the important thing was, what happened next. McCann must have been reading my mind.

"So what happens now?"

"Ah," I sighed. "That's a good question. Tell me, did Randall find out about your—ah—involvement here?"

"No," cut in Pook, "That big dumb flatfoot couldn't find a kiddy-car in a nursery. All he wanted to do was keep getting an eyeful of me. And I gave him plenty to look at."

McCann turned on her sharply.

"How many times do you need telling? Randall ain't dumb. He looks sleepy, and he talks kinda tired sometimes is all. On the murder squad they don't keep dumb sergeants."

"He's right, Pook. Don't let Randall fool you with that bumpkin routine. Still, he didn't find out about you?"

I spoke again to McCann. He shook his head.

"Not so far. You gonna tell him?"

There was something wrong with his approach. The McCann I knew was all aggression and bounce, forcing things and people into the shapes he required. Now here he was asking.

"I have too much to do to run police errands," I told him evenly.

"Of course, if they want you for a couple of axe murders, or like that, it might be different."

"Nothing like that," he said indifferently. It was almost as though he didn't care whether I turned him in or not. "So you found me. What are you going to do about it?"

I wondered how much I ought to trade for whatever he might know.

"I'll tell you the score, Legs, You know me, and you know it costs plenty to persuade me to work. I'm working."

"And? Who's picking up the tab?"

I wagged a forefinger.

"You also know I won't tell you that," I admonished. "Let's say it's big people."

"Lots a big people in town," he shrugged.

"Right. But these are big rough people. Kind of people you and I understand. They want to know who knocked off your friend Brookman. I'm supposed to find out."

He didn't contradict my use of the word friend. Not right away, that is.

"You a finger-man now, Preston? I never figured you for that kind of work."

"A man does what he can."

"And hey," he remembered. "Whaddya mean, my friend Brookman? I never heard of the guy."

I shook my head.

"I know better. You've been seen with him."

"You're crazy."

It isn't always easy to know when people are lying. But I had an uneasy feeling he could be telling the truth.

"Won't do. You were seen talking to him out at the track."

"I don't get it. This is some kinda frame. Anybody could tell a story like that. I talk to hundreds of people out at the track."

That was true. I reflected for a moment.

"Have you seen a picture of Brookman?"

"Just the one in the paper yesterday. Didn't mean a thing to me."

The one in that paper had been taken down among the rocks where they found the body. Nobody could have identified anybody from that picture.

"How about today's paper?"

"Didn't get around to it yet. Honey?"

He looked a question at Pook, and she went out into the kitchen. McCann stared at me in puzzlement, till she came back.

"Here it is, right here," she pointed.

Today's picture was the face of the man I'd seen in the morgue, after the morticians had been to work on him. McCann took the folded paper and stared, biting at his lower lip in concentration.

"Wait a minute, this guy."

He let the paper fall by his side and hung his head thinking. Then he raised his arm again and concentrated on the dead man's face.

"A horse player? Could he be a horse player?"

"He was," I confirmed.

"I think I got him. I seem to remember a guy, oh it would be a month back. This guy was into the book for a lotta dough, about three g's if I remember. Somebody asked me to talk to him about it."

I knew what that meant. McCann had to show Brookman his muscles in an attempt to shake some money out of him.

"So you had to lean on him? I'd have expected you to remember a little thing like that."

"Nah," he denied. "All I did was tell him these people don't like guys who don't pay. It makes them nervous. He had a week to find the dough, or I'd be seeing him for another little talk. That was when I was going to lump him up a little."

"I see. And the second time you saw him?"

"Wasn't no second time. He musta found the dough, I guess. Or else maybe somebody else got the job. I only saw him that one time. Yeah, I think this is the guy."

"Who did he owe money to?"

McCann hesitated.

"I don't think I'm going to tell you that. It was business. If I told you who it was, you could get to figuring that was the guy had this Brookman knocked off. That would make me kind of a stool-pigeon. This I don't wanta be."

It was a fair answer. It fitted the few facts I had, and it fitted what I knew of McCann's attitude to life. All this time, Shiralee O'Connor was standing with her arms folded, watching us.

"I just had one of those ideas," I said slowly. "You haven't been around much lately, Legs. Could be you're hiding from somebody."

He squared his shoulders as though he might be about to take a poke at me. I hoped he wouldn't. I was probably no match for him standing up. Sitting down, I was no match for Mickey Mouse.

"Why would I do that? You know me Preston, anybody has an argument with Legs McCann, I don't hide in no cellars."

"Not ordinarily, no," I agreed. "But this could be different. Suppose now, suppose this bookie got tired of waiting for his money. Suppose he thought he'd just knock off a heavy loser, and call it quits? If he did that, he might get to thinking about anybody who knew Brookman was in to him for the dough. And that anybody could be you."

"Nuts," he said with a laugh. "Everybody in this town knows me. I never hollered copper in my life, and I ain't about to start. I'm surprised at you, Preston, making up a yarn like that. And I'm not hiding from anybody. Pook and me, we're having kind of a vacation."

I looked at the girl for confirmation, and she nodded without smiling.

"A vacation?" I echoed. "With her working half the night?"

"She works nights, I work days mostly. If we was gonna get together one of us'd have to rest up."

That made sense. Shiralee said.

"That's right enough, mister. We tossed for it, and this bum won."

McCann chuckled.

"And she can call me that. That's what I am, living off a woman."

"Don't talk like that," she scolded. "We tossed for it, and I lost. It was the only fair thing to do."

I held up a hand. The picture of happy domestic squabbling between this girl who danced the private circuit, and the bookies one-man persuasion squad was more than any stomach could take at that hour of the morning.

"Knock it off," I begged. "What is this, an audition for a happy family series? What are you birds trying to sell me?"

McCann scowled.

"As for that, peeper, I ain't about to sell you anything. And that includes information. So why don't you button your trap and get outa here?"

"Ah," I said, with satisfaction, "That's better. That's more like the old Legs. Now I know who I'm talking to."

"You'll know in a minute if you don't get lost," he assured me.

From the way he was moving around, easing off his muscles, I had no reason to think he was bluffing. But I didn't get up. Instead I crossed my legs nonchalantly and leaned back.

"Stop using up all your wind," I advised. "You ought to be grateful to me."

"Yeah?"

"Yeah. If I wasn't such an all-right guy, I might walk

out of here and tell not only the cops where you are, but every bum in town. That way, whoever's looking for you will know where to come."

"Nobody's looking for me," he snarled, but it lacked conviction.

"Then you won't mind if I do just that. Can't hurt anybody."

I began to get up. The girl started, and put a hand to her mouth.

"Mac——" she said urgently.

McCann stood in front of me bouncing his right fist inside the open left palm. My jaw began to twitch in anticipation. Then he snorted with exasperation and turned away. My jaw was grateful.

"What's the use?" he said disgustedly. "So I belt him around, so what does it get me? I know I'm not going to knock him off. And so does he. Right, Preston?"

"I think so Legs. I never heard of you taking up that kind of work."

"Nah."

He held up his fists, gnarled and knotted, and turned them round for everybody to inspect.

"This is me. I don't go for the rods and all that jewelry. I lean on somebody, all right. If he's quick enough on his feet, maybe he gets a coupla pokes at me, too. That's fair."

Shiralee's face was a study in bewilderment.

"I don't get it, Mac. What is it you're trying to say?"

I grinned at her.

"What he's saying lady is, there's no profit in taking a swing at me. If I'm going to talk, I'm going to talk, and no punch on the jaw is going to stop me. The only way to be sure of me, is to kill me. And that is not Mc-Cann's style."

"Oh."

She nodded in such a way as to indicate she still had no idea what we were raving about. But there was something about the way she looked at him, not at all the way I'd expect a midnight fan dancer to look at any man. It was my turn to be puzzled.

"So what are you waiting for?" barked McCann. "Run away and peddle your dirt."

I hesitated.

"I don't know. Maybe not. How about it, Legs? You trade me a little information, and I'll forget I ever saw you."

"No deal," he said automatically.

"Aw Mac, honey," she appealed.

She walked across and put her arms round him.

"What harm can it do?" she wheedled. "You're all right here, have been so far. Maybe this guy can do some good, help get things sorted out. Then you'd be off the hook, wouldn't you? You can't stick in the apartment for ever."

"I ain't gonna turn into no fink," he said stubbornly.

"Nobody asked you to," I butted in. "All I need is whatever information you have."

He thought for a moment then shrugged her arms away from him.

"What kind information?"

She nodded eagerly, as though the question made everything come out right in the end. I lit an Old Favorite from the stub of the last one. I have to do something about all this smoking.

"Did you hear the radio this morning?"

"No."

"Then open up that newspaper."

The paper was folded so as to show the Flower murder

with its repulp of the Brookman killing. Wonderingly, McCann took it from Pook's outstretched hand and unfolded it. Underneath the fold was the story about the shooting of Jake Martello. He took in breath quickly when he saw the picture, looking at me at the same time.

"Read it," I suggested.

His eyes scanned quickly down the page. By the time he reached the bottom, he was again chewing vigorously at his lower lip.

"It says you were there," he accused.

"Right. I'm probably lucky that isn't my picture you're looking at. Another foot to the right, and I would have collected that slug."

Shiralee took the paper from his unresisting fingers.

"So somebody shot Jake Martello. Where does that get us?"

But the words had no bite. The story meant something to him.

"All right, let's take a flyer," I said. "I'll tell you what I think. I think Jake was the one who told you to scare hell out of Brookman. I think it was his three grand. I think Brookman was about due to pay back and you probably knew it. Brookman was bumped off, the money disappeared. As soon as you heard about it, you got to thinking Jake might figure you killed him for the money, Jake's money. And you would know, we all know, what Jake would do if he thought anybody crossed him up that way. So you went missing."

"And that's the way you work it out?"

"Makes a kind of sense. Makes as much sense as any other part of this crazy deal."

He went and rested his hands on a table, leaning forward as though there was a great weight on his back.

"Where were you last night, Legs?"

He shot round quickly.

"Now, wait a minute."

"Why? You killed Brookman, stole the money. The guy after you was Jake Martello. Problem, what to do? Answer, knock off Jake, then everything is the way it was before. Except, now you have a stake." He shook his head violently, as though repetition added weight to the denial.

"Crazy, you're crazy. Why, I was here the whole time last night. I haven't been outa this place in nearly two days. Why would I want to kill Jake? The guy's a friend of mine."

"Next to a woman, nothing comes between friends like money," I told him pompously.

"No listen, will ya? You're talking crazy. What're you trying to do to me?"

"Nothing. You could be doing it yourself, hiding away like this."

He gave a resigned laugh.

"The way you stack it up, I don't have any cards."

"Not if you did it, you don't," I agreed. "And I won't do anything to help you. But if it wasn't you, you ought to have sense enough to tell me anything that might help me get you off the hook."

He looked at me, then at the girl.

"Honey, step outside and make some more coffee huh?"

When she'd gone he came over and sat down, speaking in a low tone.

"You got part of the story, Preston. I was working for Jake when I put the squeeze on this Brookman. Mind you, I didn't hurt him. It was just a first call, you know?"

I knew. Where Legs McCann came from, the first call meant a talk with the offending customer. The caller had all the trappings of violence but nothing happened. The

average welsher saw enough the first time around to persuade him he was in no need of a second call.

"And what's the part of the story I didn't get right?" I
queried.

He was speaking so low now I could hardly catch the
words.

"I want out from this business. You see, Pook and me,
we're er—we want to cut this town and start over.
Understand, I'm taking a hell of a chance on you, telling
you all this."

I nodded, and leaned nearer so I could hear better.

"You know the way it is in this business, I been around
too long, too many people know me, know my record.
And as for Pook, there probably ain't a guy in town
who hasn't seen as much of her as there is. If we was
to stay here we wouldn't have a chance. So what you
said is right, I do need a stake so we can blow."

"And Jake knows all this?"

"No, not about her he doesn't. But I told him a few
days back I was thinking of starting over in another town.
Said it was time I quit pushing my muscles around and
tried something else. In a few years I'll just be a muscle-
bound bum peddling papers or something. You've seen
it happen."

I had, and to better men than McCann.

"How did Jake take it?"

"Not too bad. Oh, he was sore at first. He always is
when he thinks anybody wants to quit on him. But I've
done all right for Jake, and finally he saw it my way.
What he did say, I'd have to quit the collecting work
right then. I didn't hold that against him. You couldn't
expect him to send me out collecting all that money like
I was, knowing I was getting ready to quit town. In his
place I'd have done the same thing."

"I see. And then when one of his customers was

bumped off, you figured he might decide you helped yourself."

"Yeah. I was having a drink in a bar, and some of the guys heard this news and I got out of there fast before Jake came looking."

"But why in such a hurry?" I wanted to know. "Jake's known you for years. Why would he think you crossed him up?"

"Jake don't do a lot of listening once he makes up his mind. I'd probably lose all my teeth before I convinced him. And I do have money, cash money, just like was taken off this guy. I can't put it in no bank, I carry it around. And that wouldn't make it no easier explaining to Jake. Besides, maybe I don't get the chance. Maybe some young punk knocks me off without a lot of chatter, just to make himself a name with Jake."

With ordinary people, the kind of reasoning McCann was promoting would make little or no sense. But he wasn't talking about ordinary people. He was talking about a different world, a tight compact little world where the values took on alien shapes. To me, it made that kind of sense.

"O.K. so what do you do now?"

He looked at me speculatively.

"That would about depend on what you do."

"I'm going to forget about you. I won't tell the law, and I won't tell Jake. I came here to talk to a lady named Shiralee O'Connor. I talked to her, and that's all I know. But I'm going to ask a favor."

"Try me."

"This thing is getting a little rough. Two killings and a third attempt so far, and no telling what comes next. If I get in a spot where I could use a little support, maybe I could call you, huh?"

He held out his hand and we shook solemnly.

"You got yourself a deal, Preston. And good luck to you. I'm like to go nuts if I stay around the house much longer."

I left then. At the sound of the door opening, Pook appeared from the kitchen and smiled at me tentatively. I nodded what I hoped was some kind of encouragement, and went out.

CHAPTER ELEVEN

It was time I showed my face at the office, and from the look on Florence Digby's face when I rolled in, she thought so too.

"Morning Miss Digby. Anything going on?"

She stopped typing and looked at me severely.

"Nothing so important that you need have troubled yourself coming in Mr. Preston. Heaven knows, I have enough practice at dealing with all the mail and answering callers. It hardly seems fair to bother you with all these little details."

I mumbled something about being busy and picked up the newly-opened mail. I'm not any fonder of criticism than the next man, particularly the brand handed out by La Digby. Because the plain fact is, and we both know it, she can run the place perfectly well whether I'm there or not.

The mail was my usual bag of wanted notices, insurance company circulars and advertising. There was one guy who was finally prepared to reveal the truth behind the Lindbergh kidnapping. I hadn't had one of those in months. Handing it to Florence, I said

"Another nut. We'd better send it along to headquarters like all the rest."

"The letter is already typed ready for signature, Mr. Preston."

I might have known it would be.

"Any callers I ought to know about?"

"A woman called, a Mrs. Prince. She wouldn't discuss

the matter with me. Said it was something you would know about personally."

She let me know, by the inflexion on that "personally", that she entertained the darkest thoughts about Mrs. Prince and me. Florence always creates fantasies about any woman who crops up in my business.

"Am I supposed to call back?"

"I told her I knew little of your movements, but if you did find time to come into the office today, I would tell you she called." I went through into the inner room and closed the door. There were a few papers on the desk, some for signing, some just for information. It didn't take many minutes to clear those, then I put my feet up on the desk and lit an Old Favorite. The Brookman thing had me puzzled. Ordinarily, I'd still have a few places where I could go and make noises. The kind of noises that persuade people to tell me things, or get tough, some kind of reaction.

But with this one I was fresh out of places. And names. The only thing seemed to be to go through the whole process again, and it wasn't a prospect that appealed. I lit an Old Favorite and pulled the telephone towards me. I had to wait a minute or two before the receiver at the other end was lifted. Eve Prince said

"Hallo?"

"This is Preston, Mrs. Prince. Understand you called my office."

"Why yes, hallo Mr. Preston. I simply wanted you to know I did as you suggested. My lawyer speaks very well of you, and I wanted to apologize for being so foolish."

"You weren't foolish," I assured her. "You did the right thing. It doesn't pay to trust everybody who comes banging on the door. Say, if you're not too busy I'd like to have another talk."

She hesitated.

"Well, I have an engagement this afternoon," she said doubtfully.

"This won't take long. I don't think I should call at your house again, and the police sometimes watch my office, just out of curiosity. Perhaps we could make it a quiet drink somewhere? The whole thing wouldn't take thirty minutes."

"Oh. Well, perhaps that would be all right. Where do you suggest?"

"You know the Esperanza? It's a couple of miles out on Highway Eight?"

"Yes. Or rather, I've been past the place."

The correction was to make it quite clear that Mrs. Prince was not on first-name terms with every saloon in town.

"Fine. I'll see you out there in——" I looked at my watch——" fifteen minutes?"

"Very well. But I really mustn't stay too long."

It was a little after one when I pulled in outside Rancho Esperanza. Nobody gets any prizes for guessing the place is done out in old Spanish California style, plenty of white pillars and black iron grillework on view. Inside it was cool, and I perched thankfully on a tall stool by the bar. The jockey wore a frilled shirt with a string tie and his face looked familiar.

"Hi, Mr. Preston. Long time etcetera."

I puzzled, but not for long.

"Tom. Tom Golding."

"Right."

We shook hands, but there was still something wrong about him. Then I had it.

"It's your hair," I exclaimed. "Your hair ought to be brown."

He grinned self-consciously and patted at his shiny black locks.

"Mr. Preston, whoever heard of a Spanish waiter with brown hair? You want the job. you gotta look Spanish. You wanta look Spanish, you need black hair."

"Well, if the job is worth it," I grinned. "Pretty busy?"

"Not daytimes. We get a few people in, mostly guys meeting other people's wives. You know, we're kind of off the track out here. People can have a quiet chat with nobody around. Nights though, that's different. Man, this place really swings then. You wanta sit on that stool tonight, you better be here good and early."

I ordered some scotch with a lot of ice and Tom did his usual professional job of serving it up. As I was the only customer in the place I didn't have to feel guilty about taking up his time.

"Last time I saw you, you were working at the old Grease Paint Pot on Malabar. Something go wrong down there?"

He grimaced, as he polished away at a glass with a snow-white cloth.

"Places change, Mr. Preston. You remember the Pot, we used to get real movie people, television people, like that. Always a few faces around down there, and it was, you know, always something going on. Then suddenly they don't come any more. We always had our share of phonies around, but nobody took no notice of them. All of a sudden one day, it's all phonies. Guess they drove the real celebrities away. So I figured it was time to move on. You know me, I never could stand those dead beats."

I knew what he meant. Bartenders have their own methods for dealing with drunks, troublemakers and phonies, but even among bartenders Tom had a reputation. Then there was the sound of a car pulling up outside. A door slammed and there was Eve Prince coming through the door. Today she wore a sleeveless lemon dress that set off the deep tan, and her black hair was pulled back from her face and tied behind. She walked with a free swinging grace, and I began to regret she already had an engagement for the afternoon. Behind me, I could sense Tom watching her too, and I didn't blame him.

"Am I late?"

She smiled, one of those smiles that made people forget how long they'd been waiting.

"Not at all, I just got here. May I get you something?"

"Thank you. Could I have some gin, with ginger ale and ice?"

"Tom."

He was already busy. I led her to a table by a window, where we could look out into the paved garden where the fountain played. Tom brought her drink across and we raised our glasses.

"What shall we drink to?" she asked.

"To our better understanding?"

She smiled slightly and we sipped at the cool drink. She looked through the window.

"This is nice. You bring all your suspects out here?"

She was a different woman from the one I'd talked to before. This one was completely calm and self-possessed. And very attractive.

"No," I admitted. "Only the females. And who said anything about suspects?"

"Wrong word," she corrected. "But you did say something about another talk."

"Yes."

She refused a cigaret, I didn't. The blue smoke hung lazily in the still air, and I leaned towards her so my words wouldn't carry to the bartender.

"You said Brookman once mentioned he had a girl friend who was a dancer."

"Yes, it was just one of those little remarks that stick in the mind."

"Uh huh. Now I want you to think very hard, because it could be important. Did he say anything else about her, any little thing at all?"

She pondered for a while, then slowly shook her head.

"No. No, I don't think so. Remember, my conversations with that—that person were not quite what you could call social occasions."

"I understand. If he'd mentioned a name, you think you might recognize it?"

"I don't know. I doubt it. In fact, I don't remember that I ever heard him mention anybody's name at all."

I was disappointed.

"So if I said a name, it wouldn't ring a bell?"

"Sorry. Of course, you could try."

"How about Shiralee O'Connor. Or he might have called her Pook."

"O'Connor. No. No, I'm sorry."

That was half of my stock of dancer's names. But I still had one left.

"Serena Fenton," I said.

"Serena? What an unusual name. No, I'd have remembered that—wait a minute."

I felt quick hope while she searched her memory.

"Serena Fenton," she repeated slowly. "Isn't that the name of the girl who fell from a window last night? The one they wrote about in the papers this morning?"

"Yes, it is," I confirmed.

"But I don't quite understand. You're surely not suggesting any connection between that unfortunate girl's accident, and what happened to him, to that man?"

She seemed quite upset at the idea.

"It's a possibility, but no more than that. And you can't think of anything Brookman said that might give me a lead?"

"I doubt it. I've been thinking awfully hard after what you said, but mostly he just talked nonsense. I think he was unbalanced you know."

"Really? Why?"

She made a face.

"Well, you would hardly call our—I was going to say relationship—our connection, you'd hardly call it social. It was a straightforward question of handing over money. And yet he insisted on talking a lot, all about himself, and all nonsense."

"What kind of nonsense?"

"He used to brag a lot. He was always saying what a great favorite he was with the girls. Women know about things like that, Mr. Preston. That little—er—that man would have been lucky to get any woman to look at him twice."

"I see. What else did he brag about?"

"He always claimed he was a poet. I never believed him till I read it in the paper. Used to say he was an undiscovered great artist, the kind of thing one hears all the time from frustrated people of little or no talent."

My drink was getting low in the glass. I didn't want to order another, because any interruption to the conversation might serve to remind Eve Prince she was due somewhere else. Not that it did me any good, because just then she looked at her watch.

"Heavens, I must fly. I warned you I couldn't stay long."

"I'll walk with you to the car."

I signalled to let Tom know I'd be back, and walked beside her out into the sudden afternoon heat.

"I have to ask you one more thing, and please believe I don't want to upset you."

She gave my arm a quick squeeze.

"I believe that already."

I took a deep breath, and hoped she'd go on thinking that way.

"The time you told me about, the time those pictures were taken."

Her face went very straight, and she stared at the ground as we walked towards the car.

"Well?" she asked quietly.

"Do you happen to know the name of the man who—er—who was doing, well, the man who was involved?"

"No."

"You told me he was big, but that's all you told me. How big, for instance, as big as me?"

She looked sideways at me appraisingly.

"Bigger. Not taller perhaps, but much broader. He was —ugh—like an ape."

And I wasn't going to get any more no matter how hard I dug. I'd experienced that kind of thing before. Eve Prince had blotted him out of her mind as a person, and his place was no more than a large, shadowy, dread.

"And Somerset? Did you ever see him again?"

"Yes," she said reluctantly. "I met him at an art gallery a month or so ago. There was a private showing of quite a promising painter from San Diego, and I was invited. He was very decent about it when we were introduced. He pretended he'd never seen me before. I was grateful."

We were standing by her car now, a small red coupe. She held out her hand formally.

"Well good-bye, Mr. Preston. Thank you for the drink. I'm afraid I haven't been very helpful."

"One never knows in this business," I told her. "Maybe in a day or two some quite small thing you told me might help to explain a whole lot of other things I don't even know about yet."

"I hope so."

"Oh, and Mrs. Prince——"

"Yes?"

She paused with her hand on the starter and looked up.

"I was wondering whether we could have another drink sometime, and talk about something more pleasant?"

She nodded and smiled.

"I think I'd like that. So I'll make it au revoir."

I watched the little car out on to the highway, then went back inside. I took my glass up to the bar, to find Tom watching me apprehensively.

"Gee Mr. Preston, I never meant no harm. I mean, naturally any friend of yours is O.K. Sometimes when I talk about those other bums I say more than I oughta."

I looked at him in blank astonishment.

"Tom," I said carefully. "I know it's a very hot day, but I don't have the slightest idea what you're talking about."

He didn't believe me.

"Sure you do, no need to be polite. I mean about the lady. Honest I wouldn't have said——"

"Tom," I interrupted firmly. "Just tell me slowly what it was you wouldn't have said."

"Why about that crowd that finally took over the Grease-Paint Pot, the crowd that caused me to change my job. I mean they wasn't all that way. Some of them, one or two anyway, was real nice people."

Now I was beginning to get the point.

"Are you telling me the lady who was just here——?"

"Sure. I figured you'd know. Sure. She was in there all the time."

"I think I'm going to need another drink," I told him. "Did she used to be with any particular crowd, anybody you could lay a name to?"

He looked at me as though he thought it was a funny question.

"Why sure. Naturally I can. You know that good-looking young guy hangs around with Jake Martello and those?"

"Like an overgrown college boy, you mean? Hamilton?"

"Sure, that's him, that's the guy. Clive Hamilton."

He said it with satisfaction at having got it right. I looked across at the table where she and I had been sitting five minutes before.

"Not Clive, Tom. Clyde. The guy's name is Clyde F. Hamilton."

The drink tasted stale and flat.

CHAPTER TWELVE

I went down to the hospital. A long time ago I learned not to bother the people at reception. They can usually come up with some perfectly good reason why I shouldn't go in, and that doesn't get me anywhere at all. These days I always walk straight through, with a set face as though I'm on some urgent hospital business. They have so many people who have every right to be there. they don't even bother to look up most of the time.

Today was all right. There was just one girl behind the reception desk, head bent busily as she scribbled at some of the eternal records they have to maintain. The pretty brown hair made me wonder what kind of a face went with it, but in the circumstances I was prepared to make the sacrifice.

All the tough cases like Jake Martello's were kept at street level. The crash victims, attempted suicides, gunshot wounds and so forth. This had the double advantage of quick access for the incoming ambulance, plus accessibility to the hospital morgue if there was nothing the medics could do. I'd been to Monkton General often in the past, too often, and I was soon in the corridor where I knew Jake would be lying. There was no uniform on view, but that only meant there would be a man inside the room with him. This is partly for protection, and partly so that anything the victim says can be written down. All I had to do was get the guard moved so I could get a word with Jake.

At the end of each corridor was a public pay-phone. I sorted loose change and called the hospital.

"Monkton General. Can I help you?"

"Police Department. You have an officer with one of your patients, Mr. Martello. Can you get the officer to the 'phone please?"

"Certainly. Please hang on."

I hung on. Soon I heard the clacking of flat-heeled women's shoes, and a trim white figure passed me. I pretended to be deep in conversation. I watched as she paused outside a door, opening it carefully and slipping inside. A moment later she re-appeared, followed by a young policeman, and I watched the little procession pass me. Soon there was a man's voice on the phone.

"Cogan."

"Cogan, there's been a reported shooting at 1227 Lakeside. That's just a few hundred yards from the hospital, and we don't have a squad car available right now. Will you investigate?"

"But I'm watching this shooting victim here," he protested.

"Sorry. This shouldn't take a few minutes. Get a nurse to stay with him till you get back."

"Does Sergeant Randall know about this?" he asked.

"Sergeant Randall will be told," I replied severely. "These instructions are from the Captain."

"All right, what are the details?"

"Some kid fired a shot through a window. Probably no more than an accident. Just get the details, but proceed with caution. And the Captain says not to get gun happy. Get what you can and report in by telephone. If we get a squad car free, we'll send them along to help out. Your job is to get back to that hospital as fast as you can."

"Got it."

I pressed down the receiver and waited. After a short wait a girl in a white uniform flounced by and made for Martello's room. I gave her time to get settled in there, then followed and tapped gently at the door. Without waiting for a reply, I went in. She looked up, startled, from the magazine she'd picked up.

"What's going on here miss?" I asked gruffly. "There is supposed to be a uniformed officer on duty here the whole time."

"Oh—oh yes. He had a call from headquarters and had to go out on some urgent call. He said he'd only be a few minutes."

I looked at my watch impatiently.

"I haven't got time to hang around waiting. They told me he'd be here. I'll have to come back later, I guess."

She nodded, anxious not to get the good-looking young patrolman in trouble.

Stepping across, I looked down at Jake. He seemed to be peacefully asleep.

"How is he? Has he said anything yet?"

"Nothing coherent, I understand. But he's out of danger now. In a few days he can probably go home. Mind you, I'm just a second-year nurse, you'd have to get a proper opinion from one of the house men."

"I'll read the official stuff when it comes through," I nodded. Leaning over the prostrate figure I said "Jake," softly.

His eyes flickered, and I spoke again. This time he got them half-open, and he saw me.

"Hi," he muttered feebly.

"I don't think you ought to disturb him this way," said the little nurse nervously.

"Just a word," I explained. "Anything he can say now might save a lot of unnecessary work. Can you hear me, Jake?"

He nodded slightly.

"You know a girl named Eve Prince?"

A pause, then slowly the head moved from side to side.

"Have you been looking for McCann?"

Another pause, longer this time. Then a slight nod.

"You might have saved some time if you told me that in the first place," I reproved. "What about this Hamilton, you trust him?"

Another nod, followed by a sideways negative. I thought I knew what he meant.

"You mean yes and no?"

This time there was just a nod.

"Do you have any idea who might have done this to you? Anybody at all."

There was no response. Whatever Jake's private thoughts on the subject might be, they were staying that way. Which wasn't a whole lot of help to me. I noticed the nurse was taking a lot of interest, so I leaned close to his ear and whispered.

"You told me Brookman was into you for eight grand. Was that just talk money? I mean was it really less?"

He shook his head decisively.

"Really, I don't think you can talk to him any more."

The nurse was quite firm this time, and seemed to be getting ready to throw me out.

"One last thing," I said. "Jake, can I trust Rose? I mean, all the way?"

He felt so strongly about it, he didn't use signs. In a thin, croaking voice he said.

"All the way."

"Well, I'll come and see you again. You're going to be O.K. they tell me. Don't worry about things outside. Half the town is rooting for you."

He managed a feeble grin, and I turned away. It was

time I was moving in any case. I didn't care for an interview with an irate policeman.

"Thank you nurse," I told her politely. "You'll be sure not to leave him, till the officer gets back?"

"You may be quite sure of that. And now, if you don't mind."

She looked pointedly towards the door and I went through it with a grin.

At the hospital entrance I met a red-faced patrolman coming in at the run. He didn't pay me any attention, and I didn't hang around for him to come looking. Instead I went to Eddie's Bar and Grill for one of his famous salt beef sandwiches and a mug of beer. Eddie's is one of my favorite spots, because apart from the sandwiches, there are usually one or two people around I know. Especially newspaper people. They seem to have a special affinity with bars in general, and in particular bars where the salt beef sandwiches come highly recommended.

Today was no exception. I saw one or two reporters around, but they weren't the ones I wanted to see. I managed to find a corner where I could watch the door. Today was Tuesday, and with luck, Tip Brannigan would be in. Brannigan covers the crime beat for the Record, and though that particular sheet is no favorite of mine, it didn't change the fact he had the best crime nose in town. Sure enough, when I was half-way down my second beer, he came in through the door. I managed to catch his eye and wave him over. He nodded to show he'd seen me, collected his order and brought it to where I was sitting.

"Well well, the poor man's Sherlock Holmes. Shouldn't you ought to be out looking for clues?"

He took an enormous bite of the sandwich, and sat munching happily away.

"Not me," I hedged. "I keep away from the real crime,

leave all that stuff to you guys. With me it's just missing jewelry, runaway wives, stuff like that."

"Ha, ha," he said between bites. "Not what they tell me. Not what they tell me at all."

"And you? What about all these killings going on all over town? I'm surprised you can find time for these big lunches."

He mopped at his mouth with a huge handkerchief, then dipped his nose into the foaming beer.

"Man that's good," he announced. "You know, I've had practically no sleep in thirty-six hours."

"Insomnia?"

He snorted derisively, and helped himself to an Old Favorite from the pack I'd carelessly left on the table.

"What's with all the shadow-boxing?" he demanded. "You read the papers. You know what I'm doing."

"Let's say I could probably make a guess."

"I'll bet you could. Matter of fact, I'm sort of glad I ran into you. How about making with a little truth. You know, those facts you have you didn't tell Randall about."

"I told him all I know."

"Yah. It's only natural you should be the one standing next to Jake the Take when they blasted him. What were you talking about?"

"Now, let's see. I think I said it was a fine night, and if I recall it right. Jake said it sure was. Then somebody out in the fine night put the blast on him, and that was the end of the conversations."

Brannigan shrugged, and flicked ash on the floor.

"Naturally, if you don't want to cooperate with the press——"

"If I knew who shot him and why, I'd be down at headquarters telling Randall," I returned evenly. "I'm not the kind of hero to keep that information to myself. The guy might take it into his head to put me away too."

He nodded eagerly.

"Boy, yeah. That would make a swell story. I could get most of a page out of you, with all those little things you been mixed up in all these years. Yeah. A honey."

"Thanks for the interest," I said bitterly. "Maybe I should carry a little card saying 'in the event of my violent death, first contact Brannigan of the Record'."

"It's a thought, a generous thought."

I took a sip at the beer, and he was watching me shrewdly as I did so.

"In any case," I countered, "That's just a little shooting. I mean Jake's not even in any danger. I would have thought you'd be far more interested in that guy, the one they tossed over the Point. And the girl yesterday. The way I read it, those two could go together, and that's more of a story in your line."

"Ah," he flapped his hands in dismissal. "A two-day wonder. A nobody guy, and a dame who seems to be a piece of genuine flotsam. There's no public appeal. I have to have names, big names. Or a nice little vice ring, something to drag the public in. I mean the girl wasn't even assaulted.

"And who said she was murdered?"

He slipped the last question in casually, but years of dealing with policemen and reporters has accustomed me to the oblique approach. I looked suitably wide-eyed.

"Why nobody. At least nobody said so in as many words, but reading between the lines I assumed there was a connection between the two deaths."

He watched to see if I was bluffing, decided I wasn't.

"Well, there could be I imagine. But it doesn't matter one way or the other. There's no romance, like I said. Characters like that get knocked off every other day.

This is kind of a rough old town we have here. Next week, who knows? Maybe just a head in the stock yards. Just a head, all by itself. Then the body starts turning up all over the city. An ear in the mayor's mail, a leg left on the steps of City Hall. Now, that would be something. A man could get his teeth into a story like that."

I shuddered in mock horror.

"You ought to be writing screenplays for B horror movies," I told him. "Pity about the girl, though. Nice looker."

"Aren't they all? Nobody knocks off the frumps. If they do we don't bother to print. Did you see her?"

"Just once, somewhere. Nice."

"Yeah. I thought there might be something there. You know, this Hugo Somerset is kinda wierd. But if he was paying the tab, there's nothing to show it. She had private money."

"One of those," I sneered.

"How's that?"

"It seems to be that half the unattached dames in this town have an allowance from dear old daddy. He usually owns a complex of factories back east, or he's a big plantation owner in the south. None of them ever seems to come from ordinary homes where people have to work for a living."

Brannigan grinned and stubbed his cigaret. It was only half-smoked, but he could afford it seeing it was mine in the first place.

"My my, we're a touch bitter today. You don't have to tell me about those dames. Finding out something close to the truth about them is part of my stock in trade. I've seen 'em all. Old Southern colonels, big tycoons, Wall Street brokers. They always turn out to be running a drug store in Squaresville Minnesota in the end. No, this one was the genuine article. Big New York family.

There'll be a lot of questions asked when the big lawyers get here."

"Big lawyers?"

And I didn't have to pretend to look interested. The reporter chuckled.

"You're pointing like a bird dog. Maybe you catch the scent of a fine fat fee in the distance? Forget it Preston. Those guys won't go for any one-man outfit. They'll most likely bring in some big firm from L.A."

"I don't know," I dissented. "It's my town, I know people. Can't beat the local man, you know."

"No, I don't know. So you know a few people. Those guys'll bring money, fat folding money. That kind of money knows every people." Which was true. By tomorrow, or the next day at latest, I was going to find myself tripping over private operatives by the dozen. As if that wasn't bad enough by itself, it was just possible they could tie me far enough into the caper for Randall to be able to slap some kind of rap on me. Time, it seemed, was fading fast away.

"You got any more good news like that?"

He finished the last of his beer and got up.

"Nope. And if I had, I wouldn't tell you. Way I hear it, you don't even read the Record."

"No point," I shrugged. "I get all your stuff in my own paper the day before."

He flipped a cheerful hand and was gone. It was cool in the bar, but all the action was out on the sun-baked streets, and if I was going to earn a living it was time I got on with it. I made for Charlie Martello's apartment. He was there, shirt-sleeved, and showing thick black hair all over his arms and from his unbuttoned collar.

"Kinda soon for a return visit. You got something?"

"In this business I never know," I admitted.

"Take the weight off and get it said."

There was nobody else on view. I looked questioningly at the other closed doors.

"Where's the squad?" I asked.

"Out," he ejaculated. "Places. Talking to people."

"Uh huh,"

I mopped at my face with what started out as a white handkerchief, then stuffed the soggy rag in my pocket.

"It's a hot one," I observed sociably.

"For weather reports, I got television and radio," he said tartly. "Just come up with whatever you got."

"I have to make a condition."

"Conditions?" he queried darkly. "That don't sound to me like a guy on the up and up. Try holding out on me Preston, and you'd be sorry."

"Hear me out. First of all, you heard what Jake said, he trusts me."

"I heard him. I also seen him down at the hospital with some iron in his chest."

If I was going to get through to this big brawler, I'd have to try another tack. I took a roll of bills from my pocket.

"Either I'm in or I'm out. Here's Jake's money. I had to spend a little, not much. Tell him I'll give him a note of what I did with it. My time he can have for nothing."

I put the roll on the table.

"Wait a minute."

He sat glowering at me, thick beads of perspiration rolling down the blue cheeks.

"You're quitting? Why?"

"I'm working for Jake. He knows me, he trusts me. We have one special thing in common. Our word is good in this town. If you're standing in for him, you'd better get somebody you can trust."

I got up to leave. He continued to stare at me.

"People don't walk out on Charlie Martello," he said softly.

"Don't talk tough to me, Charlie. Not without your goons. You're getting too old for that kind of talk. That belly is all lard, and if you need a demonstration, come and get it."

He began to rise from the chair, measuring me carefully. Then suddenly he laughed, and sat down heavily.

"Aw, what're we getting sore about? We're supposed to be helping Jake, ain't that right?"

"That's how I got into this."

"So siddown. Siddown." He waved an arm like a ham. "Let's cut out this foolish talk. And pick up that dough. Jake trusts you, O.K. I trust you. Now, spill it."

I hesitated. Then I picked up the money again, weighing it in my hand.

"I mentioned conditions."

"I don't guarantee nothing. But let's hear 'em."

"First, you have to hear me out, and not lose your temper."

"Sounds fair. It's too hot, anyway. What else?"

"If you get any ideas from what I say, anything that sounds it might lead somewhere, you keep those gorillas on a leash. I don't want their big fists fouling up my investigation."

"H'm. That's a tough one. I mean, if all we gotta do is break a few heads, why don't we get on with it?"

I sat back down again, tossing the bills from one hand to the other.

"I'll tell you why. Because I have a feeling about all this. I have a feeling there's more to it than a straightforward murder and robbery. There could be plenty behind this. Now you've been around, Charlie. What happens if everybody jumps on the front man, the one who makes the contact?"

He concentrated his mighty brain power on that one.

"Why that'd be stoopid. All the big men, the ones who put the fall guy to work, they all do a fast fade."

"Right," I nodded approvingly. "And in this case, that isn't even all. In this case, we might never even get to know who the big guys are."

"Sure. I get that. That makes sense. But who says there's any big guys? I never heard of nobody who was anybody knocking off punks for a lousy eight grand?"

"That's what makes me think there's more behind it. Now, you promised to keep your temper?"

"Yeah, yeah," he said tetchily. "Get to it."

"It's about Jake. Your brother has been making book around this village for years. He's a big operator, he's tough and he's smart."

"So?"

"The dead man, this Brookman, he owed Jake money. Did you ever hear of a guy named Legs McCann?"

He was very interested now.

"Hear of him? Why, I been tearing this town apart looking for him."

"We'll get back to that. About a month ago, Jake sent McCann to give Brookman the hard word. The guy owed Jake three grand."

"Three? Jake said it was eight——"

"I know what Jake said. But he was talking about now, this week. McCann leaned on Brookman a month ago. Think what usually happens. The guy gets warned. He has two days, three, maybe a week to get the money up. Right?"

"Sure, but I don't get it. If it was three g's a month ago, how could it be eight now?"

I was glad to see the point was getting across.

"Exactly. Jake is no fool, he knows the score. If a guy's credit is up to three, he isn't going to let him run

up a tab of eight thousand dollars. You don't get to where
Jake Martello is today making dumb plays like that."

Charlie shook his head from side to side, pondering.
With one of the huge hands he wiped sweat from his
face and rubbed it on his shirt.

"It don't make no sense," he muttered. "No sense at
all. How d'ya figure it?"

"I don't know," I confessed. "To me it doesn't make
any sense either."

"Well, I'll tell you something," he breathed. "This here
McCann has some talking to do. I figure he probably
pulled this himself. He knew the guy owed Jake money.
Yeah, I'd sure like a nice quiet little talk with McCann.
He ain't hiding out for nothing, you know."

"I do know," I agreed. "He's hiding because of exactly what you're thinking. He's afraid Jake will think
just what you're thinking. The guy's scared."

"Nah," he pooh-poohed. "He's probably down in
Miami or like that with Jake's roll in his pocket. I got
people down there watching out for him. These cheap-
skates are all the same. Get a stake and blow it. We'll
pick him up, you see."

"This is where you don't have to get sore," I reminded.
"McCann is right here in town. I talked with him today."

"Where is he?" demanded Martello.

"I can't tell you that. But he didn't do this. If he had,
he'd have done what you say. He'd know Jake would
never rest till he picked him up, and all he'd be thinking
about would be how many miles he could get between
himself and Monkton City before Jake came looking."

"Maybe he's smart. Figures to stick around and bluff
it out."

"Smarter than that. He's going to stay in his hole until
somebody finds out who really did kill Brookman."

Charlie breathed heavily and looked at me in exasperation.

"You're smart, I'll say that. All right, I won't lose my temper. Not for about an hour. Tell me about the other thing."

"Other thing?"

"Sure. You said you had a feeling this was a big operation. Why?"

"Because if it's any more than a straight robbery and murder, there has to be something else."

"Nah. Who'd wanta kill a punk like that? The guy was nowhere."

"Not quite. I know at least one person who wanted him dead for personal reasons. There could be others, many others. Because the nowhere punk, as you call him, was a blackmail artist."

I watched the differing expressions come and go on his face.

"Blackmail?" he repeated. "You're sure?"

"I talked to one of his victims, a woman. She's been paying regularly for some time, you know how those creeps are. Once they find out how easy it is, they look around for more suckers. Everybody has something to hide. What I'm trying to find out now is, who else was on Brookman's list."

"I see what you mean. Cheez, this is terrible. Here's us looking for some stick-up artist. That's tough enough, but there ain't so many of them around. But blackmail. That could be anybody in town. Some ordinary joe, a clerk, a doctor, maybe this dame you talked to. This is terrible."

I nodded.

"It certainly isn't going to make the job any easier," I agreed.

Charlie looked at me with something that could have been respect.

"Say, you're not so dumb at that. Jake said you was a smart guy. You certainly got plenty done in one day. What do you aim to do now?"

"Keep poking around. This business is one per cent brain only. The rest is split down the middle, luck and getting the feet sore. But I do have one thing I'm waiting for."

"Yeah? What is it?"

"If Brookman was killed by somebody who knew he was a blackmailer, they might try to pick up where he left off. Most of these guys you know, they keep some kind of papers. Maybe a notebook, or letters, something like that. Sometimes it's photographs. If the killer got hold of the stuff, and figured to set up in business for himself, then I've got him."

"I get it. Through the dame, huh? She'll tip you off?"

"Right. Mind, it's just a chance, but I have hopes."

Charlie stood up and paced around, thinking. I didn't interrupt.

"Preston, I gotta hand it to you. So far it's O.K. But there's one thing bothers me. If it's the way you tell it, and I ain't saying it ain't, why would such a guy wanta knock off my brother Jake? He ain't after no blackmailers. He has enough trouble with his own business."

That was the one question to which I didn't have a real answer. Instead, I answered one Charlie hadn't asked.

"That worried me for a while," I admitted, "Then I decided I was beating my brains out for nothing. If I'm right, the killer has nothing against Jake, probably doesn't even know him. But he could know about me, could know I'm getting close to him. Maybe I am for all I know. What I'm saying is, the bullet wasn't meant for Jake at all."

"Ah-h."

He let out a deep sigh and nodded.

"Could be. That just could be, couldn't it? Mind, I don't say I go for it one hundred per cent, but it just could be. And it would make the rest of your ideas stand up too, huh?"

"It would. The only thing I don't like about it is, if it really was intended for me, he'll have to have another try. Because as of now, I'm still walking around asking questions."

Suddenly, and to my surprise, he stuck out his hand.

"Good luck to you, Preston. I tell ya, since Jake got hit, I been banging my head against walls. All the help I'm getting around here it's enough to drive a guy nuts. Now, things don't look so bad. What can I do for you? You want more dough?"

I shook my head.

"No thanks. I have more than enough for now. But if I get in a jam where I could use those muscle men of yours, I'd sure appreciate it."

"You got 'em," he beamed. "Just say the word."

I left him then. I was glad he was feeling so cheerful. It should happen to me.

CHAPTER THIRTEEN

The afternoon sun was really going to work by this time. The inside of the Chev felt like a baking tin on Thanksgiving Day as I rolled unhurriedly along the Beach Road. Only a few of the really hardy characters were out there surfing and splashing around. Most people were supine on the blinding sand, with unheeded newspapers and novels by their sides. The Somerset house gave no sign of life as I pulled up outside. If there were any visitors today, they hadn't left any cars on view.

I got the same unenthusiastic response from the doorbell, and once again as the door stood invitingly open, I stepped inside. I went on through to where Somerset did his music listening, but he wasn't there. The verandah door was open, and I peeked through to see him lying full length at the side of a small pool. There was a big striped umbrella doing its best to protect him from the worst of the sun. At the sound of my footsteps he lifted one corner of the gaudy cloth that covered his face, dropped it back in place when he saw who it was.

"Ah," he greeted. "The ballet expert. Why don't you sit down?"

I looked around, but there wasn't another chair on view.

"What on?"

He sighed, and again I was fascinated to watch the last ripples of it dying away as they traversed the successive bulges of fat all down his front. Somerset was very formal today. In place of the usual skin covering, he had gone to the lengths of donning a violet pair of Bermuda shorts.

"The green stuff on the ground all round you," he explained, "is called grass. People have been known to sit on it before."

I squatted down close to him.

"Have you got the police off your back yet?" I asked.

"One never knows. They're terribly persistent aren't they? I mean one would think they can't be all that intelligent."

"One would be wrong," I assured him. "Why do you say that?"

The bright cloth floated up and down on his face as he spoke, but I had no chance to see his expression.

"They ask questions," he explained. "You tell them the answer, and then five minutes later they ask the same thing again."

"It's a technique. People sometimes forget what they said the first time around. Especially people who are trying to hide something."

He chuckled.

"Well, that hardly applies in my case."

"Doesn't it?"

The cloth moved gently as he breathed. Then he lifted it from his face and turned his head to look at me.

"Is that supposed to have some deep meaning?"

"I don't know," I confessed. "You know more about what you have to hide than I do."

He regarded me carefully from the heavy lidded eyes.

"One has the impression you have something to say."

"Let's talk about Flower," I suggested.

"Ah, that poor child," he sighed. "What do you think happened to her?"

"You're forgetting," I reminded. "It was me told you what happened."

"I don't mean that," he corrected. "I mean why would anybody want to do it, and who was it?"

"I was hoping you could help a little there. Did the police admit to you they had it pegged as murder?"

"Not in so many words, but that was the way their enquiries were directed. Of course, I could tell them little."

"Of course. But I'm a different proposition."

"Really?" he raised his eyebrows. "Why?"

"Because I know things the police don't know. I know she was more than just a casual visitor around here. They'd like to know that. I know you were waiting for somebody last night. Waiting with a gun. Not the kind of thing Randall would ignore."

"Randall? Was he the big, sleepy looking one?"

"Yes."

"I got the impression he was a lot more clever than he wanted me to think."

"You got the right impression. And he'd make a whole lot of bricks out of those little things I could tell him."

Somerset seemed to be trying to make up his mind about something.

"Then, my dear fellow, why don't you go and see him?"

"Because I'm not especially interested in making trouble for you. I'm getting paid to find out who knocked off your poet friend. It's not my job to run a one-man crime-busting syndicate."

"H'm."

He reached beneath him and came up with a tall glass which tinkled with ice cubes. My tongue stuck to the roof of my mouth as I watched him pour the amber liquid down his throat.

"Brookman was neither a poet nor my friend, but these are merely words. I gather you have something to say, to come out here on a hot day like this?"

"Right. I'll tell you what I think. I think you're running a blackmail business on the side, and Brookman was your collector. That could explain why he was killed."

The rolls of fat heaved as he chuckled richly.

"Blackmail? That's a very unkind thing to say. I imagine you didn't just pluck the word out of thin air?"

"No. What you mean is, can I prove it? Frankly, at the moment, no. But I'm heading in the right direction. It shouldn't be too long before I can."

"You really are a very interesting character. And as poor dear Flower put it herself, no ordinary flatfoot. Might I ask what leads you to this drastic conclusion?"

Hugo Somerset had been using words all his life. Mixing with phonies and assorted hangers-on had developed in him a kind of shell, and the real man seldom peeped through. It wouldn't be enough to say he was taking the situation calmly. It was rather as though we were talking about other people. He wasn't going to be bluffed into anything.

"I'm in touch with one of the people you've been bleeding. It's an old routine, the one she fell for. A few drinks at a party, some guy starts putting the pressure on, and along comes a creep with a camera. I like the switch in your system, though."

"Please tell me about it."

"In your case you come along and make like big Uncle Hugo. You save the unfortunate woman, she thinks you're some kind of a shining knight. Then you put the screw on through somebody else. It's neat. But it doesn't make me like you one little bit."

He nodded, didn't seem disturbed in the least.

"Interesting. And you're really in touch with one of my—um—victims? Could I ask who it is?"

I laughed outright at the nerve of the man.

"You're wonderful," I admitted. "And of course you don't seriously expect me to tell you. But she paid Brookman regularly. Brookman was killed. Flower promised to tell me things about him, things you didn't volunteer. But Flower was killed too. The man who hired me to dig into the Brookman thing was shot and nearly killed last night. Now, do you suppose there could just be some little connection between all those things?"

"Could be," he agreed. "In fact, the neat and consecutive way in which you describe these things, one could hardly come to any other conclusion."

"And?"

"And the only little fault I can put my finger on," he explained, "Is that you're one hundred per cent wrong from start to finish."

I tossed my butt into his pool, and watched it float untidily on the still blue water.

"O.K. Hugo, if that's all you have to say. I was kind of hoping we could do some kind of a deal. I don't think I'm really after you. But if you won't trade, I'll have to tell the cops what I know. We'll see what kind of thing they make of it."

"Wait a moment."

He rolled ponderously off the chair and fell thunderously into the pool. After one or two elephantine splashings he climbed out with difficulty, pouring water in cascades all over the grass and shaking his great head.

"That's better. Clear the head. Come into the house. Perhaps it is time we had a serious talk."

He waddled past me, shaking off spray like an artificial fountain. I got up and followed, easing the .38 in its holster in case he should decide to get rid of me. Inside, he patted ineffectually at himself with a striped towel then went across to the bar, leaving damp patches everywhere.

"Beer all right?"

"Fine."

He tossed over a can and we stood looking at one another.

"Preston, you seem to be digging up little things around and about, and of course facts are facts. Supposition however, is something else again. How far can I trust you?"

"It depends," I returned. "If I find you had anything to do with those murders, you can trust me about as far as the nearest telephone."

He nodded, as though that was the expected reply.

"Fair enough. And the blackmail theory?"

"That too. In my book blackmail is as bad as murder. Worse, in some cases. So don't let's waste any time talking deal about that."

He peeled the metal strip from the top of the can, and tipped some of the ice-cold beer down. I did the same, and it was good.

"Sit down, Preston, and let's talk for a moment."

I waited for him to sit first, on a cane chair where I could see for myself there wasn't any weapon within reach. I selected a chair without arms, where there would be nothing to restrict easy access to the ·38.

"All right, let's hear the talking."

He folded his hands across the huge stomach and pursed his lips.

"I'm going to have to tell you certain things. I don't like doing it, but there are two reasons why I shall. First of all, if you decide to go to the police, I don't see how they can fail to find out anyway. Indeed I should probably have to tell them myself to be sure of clearance on this charge of murder."

"And the other reason?"

"The other is that I think if you know the facts, it might decide you not to tell the police. I like to think— don't we all?—that I am somewhat of a judge of a man. I believe you will respect my confidence."

I set down the empty can on the floor before replying.

"Don't overplay that. In my own curious fashion I'm on the side of the law. The fact that you choose to confide in me, doesn't place any inhibitions on my right to repeat it. I'm neither a doctor nor a priest. And this isn't the boy scouts."

"At least you are honest. I know where I stand. Did you mean what you said about blackmail, about it being as dirty as murder?"

"I meant it."

"Good."

He sat thinking for a moment, and I was beginning to wonder whether he'd changed his mind. Then he spoke, quite softly, and staring at the floor. There was no flamboyance now.

"You are right about one thing. There is blackmail here. It's just that you have your casting wrong. I am not a blackmailer, Preston. I have been many things, but never that. The truth is, I am one of the people being blackmailed."

I hoped my mouth wasn't hanging open.

"Last night when you came here, I was waiting for my tormentor to arrive. I'd almost screwed up my courage for murder, but your untimely appearance destroyed whatever resolve I thought I had."

That would certainly account for the gun.

"You'd better tell me the rest," I suggested, "Anybody can say what you're saying. But if you're going to talk your way out of this you have a long way to go."

"Yes, yes. I am aware of that. For me, this is the hardest

part. This is the part where I have to put myself in your hands."

He looked across for any sign of sympathy on my face. There wasn't any.

"A long time ago," he began, "I was involved in a large robbery. A very large robbery. We got away with almost a quarter of a million. Does that surprise you?"

"I gave up being surprised years ago. What happened?"

"There were three of us. We got away with the operation itself. It was a lovely job," his eyes went dreamy. "There was no violence, no last-minute hitches it went like clockwork. A lovely job. I planned it myself, naturally."

"Naturally," I said dryly.

"You see," he ignored the interruption, "we are none of us criminals. We are ordinary people, leading ordinary lives. We had agreed to carry on as normal for at least a year afterwards, then collect our individual shares, and begin to enjoy the proceeds. We were betrayed by the most damnable piece of luck. A couple of months after the robbery, one of my partners had to have an internal operation. It was nothing really major, but of course it involved anaesthesia. You can imagine what happened."

I nodded.

"He talked his head off under the anaesthetic and you were all picked up. Say, that really was a bad break."

"Indeed it was. We were arrested within hours, and the trial was more or less a formality. Not even an idiot could have pretended to believe we weren't as guilty as hell. We each got a sentence of ten to twelve years. We were offered three to five if we told where the money was, but we had already agreed not to do that. And so we went to jail. That was eleven years ago. I served eight and a half years. One of my partners unfortunately could not survive the rigours of prison life. He died after about five years. So, you see, that left two of us to share the money in the end."

A hundred thousand dollars apiece and maybe more. It was certainly something to dream about during the years behind the gray walls.

"We were watched of course, but we took our time for some months. Then one night we recovered the money and left town with just the clothes we stood up in. In different directions, that is. I think you are probably beginning to see the end of the story?"

He looked at me questioningly.

"I imagine so. If the cops traced you in possession of stolen goods or money, they'd clap another charge on you. You'd get another sentence, a tough one with all that money involved, and this time you wouldn't have the money waiting when you came out."

"Precisely. The whole thing would have been in vain. I would have given all those years of my life for nothing. This is not a prospect to be contemplated."

"I can see that. So this blackmail you mention, this means somebody showed up in town who recognized you, and they put the bite on you."

He spread his shoulders in a huge shrug.

"Again, a piece of remarkable coincidence. This creature happened to be in the same penitentiary as myself for a time, thousands of miles from here. As I say, really very bad luck. Well, there you have it. I've been quite honest with you. Are you going to turn me in?"

I wish people wouldn't ask me questions like that. Who am I to sit in judgment?

"You say nobody got hurt?"

"I can show you the complete newspaper clippings on the robbery and the trial. You can see for yourself. I may be a thief, all right I *am* a thief, but I'm not a ruffian."

I drummed my fingers against my knee while I thought. Finally I said

"I'm not an informer. If your story stands up, I guess it's none of my business."

He inclined his head slowly.

"It would be pointless for me to try to thank you. There just aren't enough thanks for that kind of thing."

"But that doesn't get me any closer to this killer," I reminded. "What else do you know about Brookman that you didn't tell the police?"

"Nothing. Really nothing."

"And how do you explain this woman who's also being blackmailed? What happened to her happened at one of your parties. Kind of a strong coincidence wouldn't you say?"

He grinned faintly.

"You ought to come to one of my parties, Preston. Believe me, there's usually enough going on to keep a dozen blackmailers in clover for the rest of their lives. You can't honestly blame me for that."

That was a matter of opinion, I thought. But looking at it from Somerset's standpoint, I could follow his reasoning.

"This particular time you broke it up," I prompted. "You could see the girl didn't want to play, and you told the man to knock it off."

He frowned, trying to remember.

"That happens sometimes," he admitted. "Most of the people who attend these little soirees know exactly what they're doing, and I don't attempt to interfere. But if I do see the kind of thing you've described, and as I say it does happen infrequently, then I put a stop to it."

"And you wouldn't remember one particular incident?" I challenged.

He wagged his head doubtfully.

"Even if I was sober when it happened, I wouldn't have been by the time the night was over. And I sometimes hold two or three of these things in one week. To remember one little incident, no I'm sorry."

It might be a little incident to you, I thought bitterly. It was slightly bigger for Eve Prince.

"And you can't imagine what it was Flower knew about Brookman that you didn't?"

"Sorry again. As I say, I didn't own the girl. She led her own life. Mind you, I wouldn't have thought her private life would include a poor fish like Brookman."

Nor I, I remembered.

"Well, I guess that about winds it up. I can't pretend I'm not disappointed. I came here hoping to tie you into this thing on a big scale. Tell me one more thing. Who is the man who put the black on you?"

He hesitated a moment, then said

"Well, having told you so much, I suppose there's no harm in telling you that. His name is McCann. They call him——"

"I know what they call him," I cut in. "I know McCann. Seems as if it's time we had another chat."

"You've spoken to him about this?" he asked in quick surprise.

"Not about this. Not directly. I knew he was in this somewhere and he told me a beautiful story that put me right off the track. He'll be surprised to see me again so soon."

Somerset said anxiously.

"You'll remember he can do me a lot of harm? I mean, from my point of view the whole thing is a waste of time if McCann informs on me in the end."

I got up to go.

"Sorry about that. But somebody was bound to get to him sooner or later. Half the goons in town are out looking for him now. I'm one of the few people who know where he's hiding. If I can keep you out of it, I will. That's my best offer."

His face was woebegone.

"Well, I've been pretty lucky so far. Maybe it'll hold. You'll try to keep me in touch?"

"This I'll do," I promised. "If I can see there's no way of keeping the cops away from you, I'll try to get word to you. There may be just time for you to blow town."

"That's a very generous offer and I thank you for it. But I'm a little heavy for running these days. I'll just wish you every success and keep my fingers crossed."

I left him there, a great mountain of a man waiting for events to catch up on him, events over which he no longer had any pretence of control.

My case was different. It was up to me to make events happen if this thing was ever going to come out right. If I'd known what the end would be, maybe I'd have quit right then.

CHAPTER FOURTEEN

Shiralee O'Connor had changed these past few hours. She wore a chiffon house robe caught at the throat by a diamond clip, otherwise swinging around her like a cape. Underneath there was a black halter bra and tight black hip length toreador pants. This was the girl in the photographs, and I could see where Legs McCann would be wanting to stay around. She gave me a slow smile, angling herself provocatively against the door.

"So soon? I thought you'd be back, but I ought to warn you he's still here."

"That's too bad. Still, as I've come this far, maybe I should have a word with him."

"Come on in."

She was very close to me as we entered the apartment. The smell of her was all around me like a warm night in a harem, and I tried to remind myself of why I'd come.

"Hey McCann, there's a man here to see you," she called.

I wasn't sure whether she was standing between me and the strong sunlight from the window by accident or design. The reason didn't matter, the effect did.

"I'm the one over here," came McCann's voice.

Reluctantly I looked away from the floor show. He was dressed ready for the street, except he wasn't wearing a jacket.

"Didn't expect you back so soon, Preston. You got some news?"

"In a way. Seems as though I didn't get the whole story

last time we talked, McCann. I can't operate if people don't level with me."

He looked puzzled, and switched his gaze to the girl, who shrugged and shook her head.

"What're you driving at?" he demanded.

"A little matter of blackmail. I wouldn't have pegged you as that kind of a rat, but we learn all the time."

"Blackmail."

He said it softly, but without any inflection of surprise.

"That's the word," I agreed. "Seems there's an old buddy of yours, you served a little time together. You found him here in Monkton and put the bite on him. It's called blackmail."

McCann was shifting his weight from one foot to the other, as though he could be getting ready to rush me any minute.

"It wasn't like that," he muttered. "I told you I wanted stake money for out. We have to blow this city, and that takes dough. I hadn't got any, he had plenty."

"That doesn't change anything. In any case, it's not my concern. What is my concern is what happened to Brookman and the girl Flower. And that's where I imagine you have more to tell me."

"I don't know nothing about all that," he said doggedly.

Shiralee decided that my tone wasn't friendly enough to qualify for a free show. She gathered the transparent robe pointedly but uselessly around her, and went to sit in a corner.

"It doesn't stack up Legs, not any more," I told him. "This morning I was inclined to believe you, keep you away from the sharks. Now I don't feel that friendly. You said you had to talk to Brookman when he owed Jake three grand. That was a month ago."

"Well, what about it?"

"This about it. You knew Brookman, knew what he

looked like. Why should Jake bother to send a different man the second time? No, it was you he sent. You said yourself you were out for a stake. I think you found one. I think Brookman offered you the money. You took it, then blew his head in and dropped him over the Point."

"Wrong," he said menacingly, "And I'm getting so I don't like you any more."

"I'm bleeding. It accounts for Flower's murder too. She'd seen you at the Somerset place, when you pressured him for money. Somerset may have told her you worked for Martello, I don't know, it'll all come out now. She wanted to tell me something, she arranged to meet me. When I got there, somebody beat me over the head and pushed her out of the window."

He sneered.

"What a yarn. There isn't a copper in town would swallow it. If I had pushed her out of that window, why didn't I make a nice neat job and push you out for an encore?"

I lit an Old Favorite to show how calm my nerves were.

"That worried me for a while. But I came up with an answer for that, too. I'm a fair sized man, take a lot of heaving and pulling to get me far enough from the floor to shove me out."

It was McCann's turn to sneer.

"I could do it easy. You want a demonstration?"

"No," I demurred. "I know you could. But Lady Godiva over there, she couldn't."

There was quick alarm on his face.

"What're you saying?"

"I'm saying it wasn't you killed Flower. It was Shiralee, Pook to her friends. I was too heavy for her, so I had to stay on the floor."

"Now you wait a minute buster," ejaculated the girl, with fear in her voice. "You can't pin this on me."

"Sure I can," I assured her. "But I don't have to try. Ten minutes after I leave here, you'll find both the cops and the Martello crowd on their way. Whichever gets here first, is a matter of chance. It makes no difference to me."

While talking to her I hadn't taken my eyes off McCann. He was the one I had to watch. Now he said

"You took an awful chance coming here with this kind of stuff."

"No," I pooh-poohed. "I don't think so. You're not able to do a thing about it. You're not carrying a gun, I can see that. I have one right here."

I patted at my arm and smiled.

"So have I," gritted Shiralee.

I turned quickly to see the small silver-plated automatic in her hand, the half-opened drawer beside her. I thought quickly about trying for the ·38, but I wouldn't have had a chance. McCann came close and said

"Hold the hands way up Preston. Honey, if he blinks, let him have it."

"Don't worry. It'll be a pleasure."

McCann looked at me with disgust.

"I oughta knock you off right now for what you're doing to me."

"No," said the girl sharply. "We're in enough trouble as it is. We'll put him where he can't do any harm till we're clear of town."

"You heard what the lady said," McCann told me reluctantly. "I hope you have lousy dreams."

The door bell clattered. Shiralee jumped up in alarm.

"Answer it," hissed McCann. "And you Preston, shut up or you're dead."

He took the gun from the girl and nodded to the door. The bell rang again. She went and stood beside it.

"Who—who is it?"

"Miss O'Connor?"

"Yes."

"My name is Hamilton, Miss O'Connor. Like to talk to you for a minute."

"I was just taking a shower," she called. "Could you come back later?"

"It's pretty important. I'll wait while you get dressed."

She came back to where we were standing. All I had to do was shout and Hamilton would burst down the door. But I had no relish for two or three nickel plated slugs in my belly.

"Fire escape," hissed McCann. "Get busy."

Then he transferred the gun to his left hand.

"This is a pity," he murmured, "I was going to have a little fun with you."

He sank a vicious right into my middle. I gave a great whoosh of agony and as I doubled up he grabbed the back of my head with both hands and smashed my face down on to his upraised knee. A warm red blanket settled over me and that was all I knew.

There was something cold and wet on my face. I scrabbled at it with limp fingers. Somebody laughed. Painfully I forced open an eye and found myself looking up at Clyde F. Hamilton. He grinned cheerfully.

"Why Mr. Preston, you really do drop off at inconvenient times. If you had stayed awake you might have prevented those characters from taking off."

I didn't like Hamilton, and I liked his jokes even less. Groggily, I sat upright. It wasn't a very good idea, because the room seemed to be having difficulty in keeping still.

"They got away huh?"

"Thanks to you, yes. But they won't get far," he said off-handedly.

"Don't be too sure," I told him. "They have a roll. There isn't just the money McCann got from Brookman. There's also a stake he got from a little blackmail on the side."

Hamilton's eyes glittered.

"Blackmail too, eh? My my, they are a busy pair. But they won't get out of town. Jake's boys have been watching ever since yesterday, and this morning I brought the police in too."

"Police? You think Jake will like that?"

"I don't know. Probably not. He'd like it a lot less if these two young lovers got clean away. Anyway, it's my responsibility."

I was thankful it wasn't mine. The Jake Martellos of this world do not normally welcome police involvement in their little activities. But maybe Hamilton had not been around long enough to be blamed. And, as he reasoned, the main idea was to prevent McCann and the girl leaving town.

"Well," I said resignedly, "What do we do now?"

"We wait," replied Hamilton. "Or rather, I wait. Jake wouldn't hold it against you if you ducked out now. You've done well. You smoked out the people he wanted, and he can't ask much more than that. In fact, you almost got yourself killed, and I'll tell him so. Jake can be a very grateful man. You won't lose by it."

I hadn't heard Hamilton so friendly before. Maybe that was something he reserved for special occasions.

"Thanks, but I'll see it through. I've been this far, and nobody could say I don't have an interest in what happens. No point in waiting around here, I imagine?"

"Nope," he confirmed briskly, "Jake's office is the nerve center. Everybody has that number, and if there's anything to hear, that's where we hear it. So, if we're going?"

He looked at me pointedly. The look meant, if you're in this thing you're in it, and if not, say so. Because those who are in it have things to do.

"You go ahead," I told him. "I'll just rest up a few minutes and I'll be behind you."

"Right. You know where I'll be."

After he'd gone, I sat around feeling sorry for myself for a time. Then, when I was able, I scrabbled clumsily to my feet and looked around for the bathroom. All the old powers of detection came into play that time. There were three doors leading out of the room. One led to the kitchen, one to the bedroom. Even in my fuddled condition, I was able to deduce instantly that the third door would be the bathroom. That's the kind of reasoning you only get from a professional, even after he's been pushed around by an expert. The bathroom had a basin which supplied hot and cold water. I filled it with cold, loosened my tie, and dunked my head into the cool. It was a refreshing experience, so much so that each time I took my head out, I waited just long enough to recharge my lungs with fresh air, then down I went again.

A few minutes of that and I was feeling more or less normal. I was patting at my face with a rough towel when the phone blatted. At first I wasn't going to answer, then my nose got the better of me.

"Well?"

There was a man at the other end. I thought I knew the voice but I couldn't recall where from.

"McCann?" came the anxious query.

I'm no good at imitations, but you can't go wrong on one word.

"Well?" I repeated.

"This is Art. Art Green. You remember, Shiralee's agent."

That was it. I did my big McCann act again.

"Well?"

This time I was more curt than before.

"Thought you ought to know. There's been some guys here. Police type guys."

Now I had to make a more serious attempt at impersonation.

"What'd you say, Art?"

"Listen, I didn't tell 'em nothing. What do I know? Nothing. They seemed to think you knocked off those people. But I didn't tell 'em nothing."

"So?"

His voice took on a whine.

"Gee Mr. McCann, a guy has to make a living. Listen, I been sick lately. I didn't even mention the boat."

Boat. My mind leaped. It was an even bet Martello's people would not be watching boats. Nor the police, for that matter. Watching a railway station, an airport, is one kind of proposition. There are just so many ways in and out. But boats. Beaches stretch for miles, and we have a lot of beaches within a short ride of Monkton. Suddenly I needed very badly to talk to Art Green.

"Stay right there. I mean it."

That was all I said before I put down the phone. As an imitation of Leg's McCann's voice, I didn't know how it would stand up. But I wasn't in the market for auditions. I needed to catch up with a couple of killers before they left town. A few hours in a seaworthy craft could put them in Baja California, and with the kind of stake money they were carrying, none of us would ever see them again. Of all the things they'd done, it was Flower's murder that more determined me than anything else. At once, I dialled Jake Martello's office. A strange voice said

"Race Investments Limited."

"Is Clyde Hamilton there yet?"

"No. Who is this?"

"Now listen, I don't know who you are, but you're going to take a message. You are going to get it right the first time, because there isn't any room for mistakes. You understand?"

"Say what is this? Who are you, anyway?"

"The name is Preston. Got that? I'm after the people who shot Jake. Understand? Right. Now tell Hamilton this. We need a man on each quay. That's Q-U-A-Y. Got it? We need a man on each one, and pronto. McCann may have a boat. And tell Hamilton I'll see him in thirty minutes at White's Boat-House. Repeat it all back."

"If you're kidding me——" began the voice.

"Just get it wrong, my friend. Get one thing wrong, and you'll find out who's kidding. Now read it back."

He read it over and I was satisfied.

"He'll be there any minute," I announced. "See he gets that message immediately."

I was about to hang up, when the voice said

"Wait. What about the other Mr. Martello? Suppose he gets here first?"

"Tell him too. Tell everybody. But get it done."

I got out then, down into the early evening sun and the slowly cooling Chev. Within fifteen minutes I was banging on the door of Art Green, Impressario.

"Who is it?" came a quavering voice.

"McCann," I gruffed.

The door was unlocked and he opened it slowly. Seeing me, he gasped and tried to close it, but I was in no mood for those impressario moves. I slammed it open, grabbed him in both hands and kicked the door shut behind me. The small dirty man was whimpering with fear.

"Now Art, tell me about the boat," I invited.

"Boat?" he queried.

I slammed him against the wall, not too gently.

"Art, we have to understand each other. McCann and the girl are wanted for two murders. Two, Art."

To illustrate the point I banged him against the wall twice more. He shivered with fright.

"The boat," I prompted. "If I have to break an arm or a leg, or maybe both, you are going to tell me about the boat. Go easy on yourself."

He shook his head.

"Legs'll kill me. I tell you he'll kill me."

"He's all washed up Art. Everybody in town is after him. Martello's people, cops, everybody. And me. And I'm the one who's here. Where would you like me to start? Left arm?"

I grabbed the arm, putting one hand behind the elbow and exerting pressure. He screamed, more from fear than pain.

"No, wait," he gasped. "How about a few dollars? I could blow town till it's over."

I let go and looked at him with disgust. Then I took some bills from my pocket, peeled off a few.

"Two hundred. Way you live, that should last a year. What about the boat?"

"It's an old tub really. Just for coast work, you know. Fruit season, McCann usually runs a few greasers up from the south." Illegal immigrants. A favorite local pursuit.

"Name?"

"The Costa de Mar. It's beached just this side of Indian Point."

A quiet piece of coast, too rocky for all but the most expert divers and swimmers.

"Who has the concession down there?"

"An old guy named Jim. Calls himself Captain Jim.

Everybody knows him. He just makes sure things are O.K. while the owners are not there. You know the kind of thing."

I knew the kind of thing. An excuse to keep some old beach bum off the public charge.

"Art, here's some advice. And there's no charge. Grab your other shirt, if you have another shirt, and be out of town within thirty minutes. I won't tell Martello you've been holding out about McCann for one hour. That's all I guarantee. Kabish?"

He nodded feverishly.

"Gotcha. Say, I sure appreciate——"

I looked at my watch.

"Time is running out, Art."

I left him looking for the other shirt.

CHAPTER FIFTEEN

Hamilton was parked outside White's Boat-House in an open white Alfa-Romeo when I got there.

"What's it all about?" he greeted.

"You drive, I'll tell you on the way. You got a man out at Indian Point?"

"Should be by this time."

He slammed gears and I was pushed against the back of the seat as we roared away. I told him about the boat as we hurtled along the beach highway.

"Nice going," he complimented. "Very nice going."

"We could be too late," I reminded. "They had a head start."

"Maybe. But I took the distributor out of the girl's car before I went calling. They'd have to hire, or get a cab. And they know everyone's watching out for them. It's my bet they won't even make their play until dark."

That made sense. Fifteen minutes hard driving brought us to the base of Indian Point. There were ten or twelve small boats hauled up on the beach. An old guy in a dirty white peaked cap sat talking with a thickset man whom I'd seen around one of the betting parlors. He got up as we approached.

"It's here, huh?" he greeted.

"With luck," replied Hamilton. "What was that name again?"

"The Costa de Mar," I told him.

She was the fifth tub along, a faded thirty footer in bad need of a paint job. There was no sign of life. We went back to the old man.

"You Captain Jim?" I asked him.

"That's me, shipmate," he confirmed.

"O.K. *shipmate,*" I emphasized, "tell us about the Costa de Mar. Will it run?"

He cackled.

"Not now it won't. Not right now."

"Listen you."

The other man took a menacing step forward, but Hamilton waved him away.

"Why not now, Captain Jim?" he asked softly.

"No oil for the engine," he explained. "No oil, no run. Makes sense."

"Where would a man get oil?" pressed Hamilton patiently.

"From me mostly. Keep a stock back there."

He waved towards a once-white shack that stood back from the beach.

"Cash in advance of course," he cautioned.

"Sure, sure. So if anybody wants to get that old hulk out to sea, they have to come to you for oil first?"

"Don't have to," he denied. "But there ain't no point dragging them big drums all the way out from town, when they know I got 'em right here on the spot. Makes sense."

Hamilton smiled and patted him on the shoulder.

"That it does old man, that it does."

He walked away, leaving him sitting there.

"All we have to do is wait," said Hamilton. "That is, assuming they decide to come this way at all."

"Makes sense," I replied.

It would be dark in about an hour. Hamilton drove the car behind some bushes where it wouldn't be so conspicuous. We sat there, busy with our own thoughts. I looked up at Indian Point, thinking what an odd coincidence it was that the whole thing should begin and end at the same place. Thinking about a guy who wrote lousy poetry, and who ended up on the jagged rocks a couple of hundred yards from where I was sitting.

Time dragged slowly by, and the sun lay low on the sea now, shooting blood red darts across the darkening surface. I threw away the butt of my third cigaret, resolving that tomorrow I would definitely give up the habit.

"Listen," said Hamilton suddenly.

Above the soft splashing of the waves came the sound of a car, and soon headlights came into view further along the beach. Hamilton reached inside his jacket and pulled out the little black automatic I'd last seen in Rose Suffolk's office.

"Might get rough," he explained.

I nodded and produced my ·38.

The headlights stopped twenty yards away, and were switched off. A man climbed out and called out to the old man, who sat puffing at his pipe.

"Cap'n Jim, gonna need some oil." It was McCann's voice. Hamilton put a hand on my arm and motioned for quiet. The other door of the car opened now and Shiralee got out and walked to catch up McCann. She was carrying a bag.

"McCann, hold it right there," shouted Hamilton.

At the same moment, he switched on the car headlights, catching the two in the sudden beam. McCann shouted.

"It's Hamilton."

He dived inside his pocket and pulled something free. The gun in Hamilton's hand jumped once, twice. I fired at the same time. McCann screamed and clawed at his stomach. The girl shrilled with fear, and turned to run.

Before I realized what was happening, Hamilton levelled the automatic carefully and pumped two shots at her retreating back. She threw her arms out sideways and sprawled forward on to the sand.

"You lousy butcher," I snarled, "She couldn't get away."

He turned on me with lips pulled back over his teeth like an animal. For a split second, I thought I was going to get some of the same. Then he laughed lightly and put the gun away.

"But we couldn't be sure."

I felt sick. I left him to look at McCann while I walked over to the spreadeagled body of Shiralee O'Connor. It didn't take a second look for me to know she was dead. The two black holes in between her shoulder blades were not three inches apart. She looked pitiful with her legs twisted all askew, and her face half-buried in the sand. I felt cold rage at Hamilton, who had shot her down as if she were a mad dog. McCann had been different. He was armed, and somebody had to shoot first. But with the girl, all we needed to do was run and catch her.

I became aware that someone was standing close. I looked up to see Martello's other man looking down at Shiralee. In the dim light I could see the stricken look on his face.

"Holy Mother," he muttered, "She wasn't doing no harm. Jake ain't going to like this."

I straightened up and stood beside him.

"We'd better get some law in here. You know where there's a phone?"

"I'll go ask the old man," he said, glad of something to do.

I knew how he felt. Catching sight of the bag Shiralee had been carrying I went over and opened it. There was money inside. I toted it a few yards into the light thrown by Hamilton's car. For no good reason I could think of, I began to count the money. Hamilton came across.

"That's Jake's. I'll take care of it."

I turned on him viciously.

"You just keep away from me Hamilton. And don't tell me what to do. I got my stomach full of you, and I don't need more than half an excuse to ruin your nice pretty face."

He scowled tightly.

"Don't talk so tough to me, Preston. As you once said, we're both on the same side, and that's all there is between us."

I ignored him, occupying my mind with the money. There were five thousand dollars, plus a few loose bills.

"We have company," said Hamilton.

I looked to see new lights coming along the beach. It was too soon for the police, surely. A car screeched to a stop. Doors banged and men came running forward. Charlie Martello and his two hoodlums appeared in the circle of light.

He took in the picture, looking first at McCann, then at the girl. He ignored Hamilton, speaking directly to me.

"All right, let's have it," he snapped.

I told him how I found out about the boat, and how we came to be waiting. Hamilton tried to butt in at one point, but Martello motioned him to be quiet.

"When they showed up, McCann went for a gun and we both shot him."

"I see. And the girl?"

"She ran away. This maniac shot her in the back. Twice. It was the most cold-blooded thing I've ever seen."

Hamilton swung a sudden fist at me, and I'd been hoping for the chance. Ducking, I kicked hard at his kneecap. As the force of his swing took him off balance

I brought my elbow up hard into his face revelling in the soft crunch of breaking cartilage. He howled in agony, and I chopped him at the side of the neck. Then Charlie's men pulled me off him, and I stood cursing and panting, a man holding each arm.

Hamilton was doubled in pain, and when he lifted his head, there was blood all over his face. I felt exultant.

"That's enough," barked Charlie Martello. "Take their guns."

His goons took away the ·38 and fished in Hamilton's pockets till they found his weapon.

"Don't want you boys being bad friends," explained Charlie. "What's that money you have there, Preston?"

"It was in the girl's bag, but I don't understand it. Jake said he was short eight grand, but there's only five here. On top of that, I know McCann got money from a man he was blackmailing, so there should be at least ten here, maybe more."

Charlie turned to the tall goon.

"Check the car."

Hamilton was trying to repair his face with a handkerchief, but it would take more than a few dabs with a piece of linen to correct the damage I'd caused. The goon came back and whispered to Charlie, who nodded.

"Why'd you kill the girl, Hamilton?" he asked.

"I'm afraid I got excited. I wasn't thinking straight. There she was, running away. All I could think was, I have to stop her. Next thing I knew, she was dead."

"Dirty liar," I spat.

"Shut up, Preston. I don't think you're quite right, Hamilton. I have an idea you were thinking very straight indeed. With these two dead, we have a nice tidy end. Nothing loose, isn't that the way you figured it?"

Hamilton looked at him strangely.

"Alive or dead," he shrugged. "What's the difference? We've got them now. It's all over."

Charlie laughed, a low unpleasant sound.

"Oh no, it's not over yet. And it does make a difference whether they're alive or dead. Because dead people don't tell tales. And these two could have told plenty."

I looked at Charlie, wondering what was on his mind. He had both hands plunged in his pockets, and his face was grim.

"I've been filling in the time looking through Jake's books," he continued. "And I don't think this Brookman character owed him any money at all. Jake trusted you with checking the books, you with all that fine education. Jake never figured you for a four-flusher. If you said Brookman was in the red, that was good enough for Jake. But when it got too hot, when you'd put eight grand in your pocket, somebody had to get blamed. And Brookman got elected."

Hamilton's face was rigid.

"That's crazy talk," he protested, "You can't prove any of that."

"I don't have to prove anything," Charlie reminded. "I'm not a district attorney. I'm just a guy who knows what he knows. And I don't operate in no courtroom. That's why you knocked these people off, just to keep everything tidy. And you nearly killed Jake, too. It's curtains for you, Hamilton."

"No, no wait a minute," he said anxiously. "I couldn't have shot Jake. Preston will tell you. I was inside the club at the time. Tell him Preston, for God's sake."

I nodded grimly.

"Sure, you were inside. What does that prove, except you didn't pull the trigger yourself?"

"Right," growled Charlie. "There's plenty guys all over

this town, any town, who hire out for that kinda work. So what's the story?"

"Listen, now please listen Charlie, you're all excited," begged Hamilton. "If you'll just take it easy, give me a chance, I can explain."

"Go ahead," invited Martello. "Start by explaining what these two——" he indicated the two bodies—"What they did with the money. Where is it, that eight grand they got from Brookman?"

"I don't know, but give it a couple of days, maybe we can find out. You have five of it right there."

"No we don't," I contradicted. "That's black money. I don't need more than one telephone call to find out where that came from. It's my guess it's all from one man, one payment."

Hamilton's face began to work.

"But you can't judge me on this kind of stuff," he bluffed. "You have to give me a chance, some kind of chance."

"Sure. I'm a reasonable man. You tried to murder my own brother, you knocked off them two, probably others. But I'm going to give you a chance."

Martello produced a heavy automatic from his pocket.

"Now, you start running," he said softly. "And I'm gonna count clear up to three before I start blasting."

"No, Charlie," screamed Hamilton. "Preston, you can't let him do this."

"It's better than the break you gave Brookman," I told him flatly.

He was sweating with fear, and there was the knowledge of death in his eyes.

"He was just a bum," he screamed. "Nobody at all. Why——" His voice tailed away as he realized what he had blurted out.

"One," intoned Charlie.

"Oh God." Hamilton sank to his knees. "Look Charlie, try to understand the way it was——"

"Two."

"Jake's alive," he pleaded, "He's going to be all right. Just give me a break."

"Three."

Charlie's hand tightened on the trigger. I struck downwards hard at his hand and the bullet plunged into the sand a foot in front of the screaming Hamilton.

"What the——?" shouted Charlie, nursing his wrist.

The two goons moved towards me.

"No Charlie, listen." I picked up the gun. "This is not the way. We have this guy cold. Let the law do it. Use your head." Hamilton was stretched out on the beach, weeping uncontrollably. Charlie glowered at me.

"You done all right so far Preston. But this is my business."

"Sure," I reasoned. "But think man, think. You'll make yourself a murderer, and in front of all these witnesses. Even if nobody talks now, how will you like it knowing all these people are walking around loose, and any one of them could put the finger on you any time he likes? The law will deal with Hamilton, that's what it's for."

His breathing became more even, and he stared at me a full minute before speaking.

"You got a cool head there, Preston. And you talk sense. What good would it be to Jake if I got myself the death chamber over this kind of trash."

He stepped forward and swung a vicious foot at Hamilton's head. The whimpering stopped. Charlie chuckled.

"You know, this is the first time I ever waited around for the law to show."

There were lights on in front of the house, and my ring was soon answered. Eve Prince wore a long red housecoat with gold edging, and she looked good enough to eat.

"Why Mr. Preston," she greeted with a smile. "It's a little late for calling isn't it?"

"This won't take long," I assured her. "May I come in?"

"Well——" she hesitated, "Well, just for a little while." She closed the door behind me, and stood close.

"I hoped I'd see you again, but I didn't think it would be quite so soon."

I put my arms around her, and she slid into them easily. Her lips were soft and moist and I could feel her heart pounding against me. Then gently, she pushed me away.

"Easy now. You wouldn't take advantage of a poor widow lady? Not until we've had a drink anyway."

I followed her into the comfortable room I'd visited before. When was that, ten years ago, fifty?

"Scotch?"

"Thank you."

I settled down with my drink and she sat primly opposite, presumably so as not to let me get any ideas. Not yet.

"I think we'll have to be frank with each other, Mark," she said hesitantly. "I'm—I'm not just another woman."

"All right. That suits me." I set down the glass and locked my hands together on my knees. "Tell me about Clyde Hamilton."

Her face changed, and now she was worried.

"Clyde? What about him?"

"You didn't tell me you knew him," I pointed out.

"But I know lots of people I haven't told you about," she protested. "I've hardly had much opportunity yet."

"Clyde is different," I insisted. "You spent a lot of time with him at the Grease-Paint Pot. You must have known who he was, what he was. But you didn't tell me. Might have saved a lot of time. Tell me about him now."

She flexed her hand nervously on the arm of the chair. "You'll have to know anyway. He's my brother."

"Your what?"

It wasn't a very intelligent remark, but the answer was unexpected.

"Yes. I moved here a long time ago, and of course Clyde knew that. He's always been a little bit wild, and I was worried about the kind of company he was keeping back home. But he's a grown man, and it was too late to change him. Then he came here to Monkton City a few months ago, and he hadn't changed. I thought if I spent some of my time with him, had him meet some nice people, it might help. I should have known better," she ended bitterly. "Well now you know. My brother is a bad hat, Mark. Does it have to matter to us?"

"And she fixed him with a nervous, trusting smile, hoping with all her heart that Clyde's reputation would not come between her and the man she loved," I sneered.

She flushed.

"That was a pretty rotten thing to say. You'd better go."

"Aw, come on angel, there's only us watching this picture. No critics to rave about your performance."

"I don't understand one word of what you're saying," she informed me icily. "Are you drunk?"

"No. I wish I were," I said sadly. "And I wish I could leave you out of this, but I can't. Remember the little tale you told me about that wicked blackmailing Brookman?"

"What about it?"

I shook my head regretfully.

"Not true angel. Not a word of truth in it. You told a naughty fib."

"I did no such thing," she protested. "Why, I paid him——"

"Nothing," I finished. "Big fat zero is what you paid

him. That was a little tale Clyde taught you, after he pushed the poor devil off the Point."

Her face was white and strained.

"What're you saying?" she whispered.

"Didn't you know? It was your bad bad brother killed Brookman. He'd been robbing Jake Martello and marking the books so the missing money was debited to Brookman. Maybe some others too. We'll know it all when the accountants are finished with Jake's books."

"But that's ridiculous. Clyde couldn't have——"

She stopped as she saw the stony look on my face.

"But bad old Clyde says he did. He's down at headquarters right now, honey. You know what else he did? He killed two other people tonight, one of them a girl. He shot her in the back. I saw him do it."

"Lies," she blazed. "What madness is this?"

"Madness is right," I agreed.

Again she shook her head in dumb refusal to accept.

"He's always been rather wild, but this—this is——"

She passed a hand across her face.

"I know," I soothed. "It's tough news for you. But I'm afraid there's worse to follow."

"Worse?" she repeated. "What could possibly be worse?"

"Why we mustn't leave old Clyde all alone down there, must we? I know little details get overlooked sometimes, but I'm afraid we haven't quite cleared up Flower's murder yet."

"Flowers? Who is Flowers?" she queried.

"Was," I corrected. "And not Flowers. Flower. A girl whose real name was Serena Fenton. You must recall her, surely? You tipped her out of a window, remember?"

Eve went very still.

"I did what?"

"You can't have forgotten, surely. It was just a few

hours ago. I was there too. You hit me over the head with something, but I was too heavy for the window exit."

"I think you must be insane. I'm going to call the police."

She made a move to get up, sat down again when she saw the ·38 pointed at her.

"You're going to kill me," she said tonelessly.

"No, no. Just want you to stay where you are. I left word for the police to be called ten minutes after I left town. They ought to be here within minutes."

"Why are you doing this to me?"

"But angel, I'm not doing anything. I don't want you roaming around the house, wearing yourself out. Besides, I have a feeling there might be a rifle around here some-place. If there is, and it's the one that was fired at Jake Martello last night, you're a pretty good shot. And I wouldn't want to have you demonstrating on me."

She bit her lip, and sat very still.

"Don't worry too much," I suggested. "You give the jury that big sister act you gave me. With the right clothes, and the right attorney, you'll probably get away with seven to ten. There'll still be plenty of good killings left in you when you come out."

Her eyes fixed on me with implacable hatred.

"You should pray they keep me in there forever."

"Threats?" I mocked. "What happened to all the lovey-dovey?"

There was a wail in the distance on the night, growing louder.

"Mark, listen to me," she said urgently. "I have almost twenty thousand in cash right here in the house. We could leave now, right now, as we are. You have a car. We could be in Mexico tomorrow. And believe me I can be very good company."

She leaned towards me, eyes shining, lips parted, and for a brief instant I wavered. Maybe I was tired.

"Sorry, angel. I hear they have lower windows down there."

Brakes screeching now, doors slamming, men running to the house.

"So this is how it ends," she muttered.

"This is how it ends," I confirmed.

It always does.

THE END

6/99